The
ARCHAEOLOJESTERS

BOOK 1

Published by Lobster Press™
1620 Sherbrooke Street West, Suites C & D
Montréal, Québec H3H 1C9
Tel. (514) 904-1100 • Fax (514) 904-1101 • www.lobsterpress.com

Publisher: Alison Fripp
Editorial Director: Meghan Nolan
Editor: Mahak Jain
Editorial Assistant: Nicole Watts
Graphic Design & Production: Tammy Desnoyers
Production Assistant: Luckensy Odigé

 Canadian Heritage   Patrimoine canadien   We acknowledge the financial support of the Government of Canada through the Canada Book Fund for our publishing activities.

Library and Archives Canada Cataloguing in Publication

Oertel, Andreas
    The archaeolojesters / Andreas Oertel.

Interest age level: For ages 9-11.
ISBN 978-1-897550-83-0

    I. Title.

PS8629.E78A67 2010   jC813'.6   C2009-905724-7

Printed and bound in Canada.

 Text is printed on 100% recycled post-consumer fibre.

For H

– Andreas Oertel

Acknowledgements

I sincerely appreciate Lobster Press taking a chance on me – a new writer. And thank you, Mahak Jain, for making the editing process painless and enjoyable.

BOOK 1

The ARCHAEOLO JESTERS

ANDREAS OERTEL

Lobster Press ™

CHAPTER 1

"Hey, Cody, I think he caught another one," Eric said. He tried to spit the remains of a sunflower seed down the riverbank. The seed caught an updraft, hung in the air, and landed near his foot.

I sat up. I wasn't too interested in whether or not Dr. Murray caught another fish. In fact, I didn't care about the first two fish that were reeled in and promptly announced by my best friend, Eric Summers.

"Maybe he snagged a tire," I replied.

From our hideaway in the tree line, I watched the old man's back. We weren't *really* hiding from him – it was just that our observation post above the river was hard to see from down by the dock.

Anyway, Dr. Murray – retired now from some kind of doctoring – was indeed reeling in an object. We were close enough to see his line flex under the strain of whatever he had hooked. But we were too far away to see if it was anything edible. I was surprised that there were even fish left, with him hauling them out day after day.

"Yup, it's another pike," Eric announced

proudly. "Maybe a two-pounder."

"Awesome." I stretched out again in the shade, next to our bikes. "So that makes how many now? Five?" I closed my eyes and grinned.

"Nope, three. I was counting –" Eric stopped mid-sentence when he realized I was joking. "Jerk!" He spit another seed over the bank, but the updraft spit it right back into his face.

We were only six hours into our summer holidays and we were already bored. Actually, we were bored and broke. But the broke part wasn't our fault. We would have loved to have summer jobs, but when you're twelve, there's not much anyone can hire you to do. And when you live in Sultana, Manitoba – population 463 – there aren't many people around to hire you in the first place.

"I'm hot," Eric whined, bored of counting fish. "Let's go swimming."

"Where? The river's pretty much gone."

We both craned our necks and looked toward what was left of the MacFie River. The spring thaw had dumped huge amounts of snow run-off into the river. But the MacFie couldn't handle all the meltwater and had washed out giant sections of the bank. Now these eroded areas looked like ugly wounds, revealing exposed roots, earth, and stone. Since April, however, there had been almost no rain, and the river was lower than anyone could remember.

The MacFie emptied into the Red River around the bend and even that was shrinking fast. In fact, it was so low you could now see the skeleton-like spine of an old York Boat. Eric and I had checked it out as soon as we heard about it, but lost interest when we saw it. It was no treasure-filled shipwreck.

"We're probably going to have to move soon," Eric said abruptly.

"Why? It's not even that hot yet."

"No." Eric lowered his voice. "I mean, we may be moving away from Sultana."

I snapped into a sitting position. "What?"

"I heard my mom talking on the phone yesterday." Eric ran his fingers through his sweaty, blond hair and looked away. "She said that if things don't pick up at the restaurant, she's going to get fired, or let go, or whatever they call it."

"What?" was all I could think to say. My brain rapidly processed this shocking information. If Eric's mom got fired they would *have* to move because there was nowhere else to work in Sultana. We only had one gas station in town – that was where my dad worked – and one motel and restaurant, the Rivercrest. And Eric's dad had died in a car accident when we were seven and his mom never remarried. With only Mrs. Summers working, it was especially important that she keep her job there as a waitress.

I tried to swallow but my throat felt dry. It was hard to imagine Sultana without Eric. He was like my brother. Sure we looked different – Eric had blond hair, blue eyes, and freckles, and I had brown hair, brown eyes, and skin the color of peat moss. But otherwise, our interests were so similar it was like we were the same person.

"But maybe things will pick up," I said, making a feeble attempt to sound positive. "The summer has barely started."

"Come on, Cody. Get real." Eric watched with exaggerated interest as Dr. Murray unhooked his fish. "You know the only reason people come out here is for fishing, swimming, boating, and camping. And now the campground's empty."

Again, there wasn't much I could say to comfort him, because he was right. Sultana was on the dead-end stretch of a highway, and the only thing that kept it alive – if you wanna call it that – were tourists. We got the snowmobilers in the winter and the campers in the summer. But no one wanted to camp next to a muddy, stinky lake or a dried-up river.

"If only it would rain for a week. Or *something*," Eric glared at the cloudless sky. "Then the rivers and lakes would rise, and people would get their butts out here."

I stared at Eric. "Or *'something'*?"

"What?" Eric leaned against a towering jack pine.

"You said, 'or something.' We could make *something* happen."

"How are we supposed to make it rain?" Eric retorted.

"No. Forget the rain. Why wait for the weather to change? Most cars just pass right through anyway. I'm talking about making something happen here in town that will make people *want* to come to Sultana."

"What do you mean?" Eric asked.

"Okay." I took a deep breath and started over. "You know how some towns have attractions that make people visit that place? Maybe Sultana needs some sort of massive statue that people would want to come and see for themselves."

"You mean like that huge fish in Selkirk?"

"Yeah, that kind of thing. People are always picnicking there and taking photos of that steel catfish."

Eric nodded. "But a project like that takes lots of time, and probably tons of money. We need something fast – real fast."

"Yeah, you're right ..." I sighed. "It would take years to raise enough money to buy a big stupid moose, or gopher, or spruce bug, or ..."

"What about a discovery?" Eric interrupted, regaining some of his enthusiasm.

I crawled closer to the shade to escape the sun. "What do you mean?"

"What if something was seen around here that people would be interested in? Like a U.F.O.?"

"Well, I guess ... but who would believe that we saw a spaceship?" I paused to think. "We need something better. Something that will make people come to Sultana all summer long."

We sulked in silence, racking our brains for a sensible solution. Probably a quarter of an hour passed, and then Eric jumped up and paced around the small clearing. He stopped after his fifth lap and faced me again.

"How about this?" he said. "We make some kind of a Sasquatch outfit, and wait in the woods at the edge of town. Then, when we see a vehicle approach, we lumber across the highway like Big Foot. Yeah, and maybe even drag a dead rabbit. You know, for authenticity."

"That could definitely work," I said. And I meant it too. "A reporter would come to town, and it would make the papers. But do enough people believe in Big Foot that they would drive out here to look for him?"

"I suppose not." Eric resumed his pacing.

"With my luck, that first car coming down the highway will be full of crazy hunters, and I'd be shot dead. And then I'd really be in trouble. Nope, we need to get lots of people to come here. And we need them to stay at the Rivercrest and buy gas from your dad."

"What if something was actually discovered here in Sultana?" I wondered out loud. "Something so spectacular, reporters would come from all over the place to do a story about it? Wouldn't *that* be cool?"

"Very," Eric said. "But there's nothing to find around here." He indicated the general area with a flick of his head and then slumped down next to me again.

"Remember last summer when that dinosaur fossil was discovered in Morden?"

Eric nodded.

"Well, that story made the paper right away. Researchers and paleontologists came from all over the place to look for more bones. It was a big deal there and we need a big deal here."

Eric nodded some more, and sat up a bit.

"And remember when we found those arrowheads across the river?"

Eric smiled at the memory. "Yeah, that was fun," he said.

"Well, suppose we hid some artifact ..."

"... and then pretended to find it," Eric said, getting excited once more. "That would create a buzz for sure."

"Well, we don't even have to find it." I flattened a mosquito on my arm. "In fact, it would be better if we *didn't*. It would be way more believable if someone respectable found the thing we wanted found."

A smile spread across Eric's freckled face. "Someone like Dr. Murray?"

I rolled over to the edge of the bank and watched Dr. Murray repack his tackle box. He collected his fish and then labored back up the access road to his rusted yellow half-ton truck.

"Yes," I said. "Someone exactly like Dr. Murray."

We spent the next hour trying to think of something that Dr. Murray could "discover". Eric lay on his back under the pine trees with his eyes closed – he had been still for so long I wondered if he was sleeping. And I was on my stomach, staring at the river for inspiration. Every ten minutes or so, a car crossed the bridge that spanned the MacFie and I turned my head to watch it. The bridge was 300 feet beyond the dock – locals considered it to be the beginning of the wilderness.

My head started to hurt. That's how desperately I tried to think of some way to avoid Eric having to move. I didn't want him to go for selfish reasons mostly. For example, who would I hang out with? There were no other twelve-year-olds in Sultana. Well, except for Rachel, Eric's twin sister. But she was a girl and didn't really count. Though I suppose I didn't want her to move either.

Eric rolled over and broke the silence. "Do you remember what Mrs. Leavesley said about that old Pioneer spacecraft that NASA shot into space in the 1970s?"

I tried to remember what Eric was talking about, but the sun and quiet made it difficult to think about science class. "Kind of, I guess. I think she said it was the first spacecraft to leave our solar system."

"Yes." Eric clapped his hands together, pleased that I had passed his science quiz. "She also said that the spacecraft had a plaque on it with symbols, in case aliens ever found it. Then they could decipher and translate the message, figure out where earth is, and –"

"– And come here and wipe out all us two-legged meat puppets?" I laughed.

Eric ignored me. "So why can't we make a mysterious tablet, engrave it with an alien message, and then hide it?"

"You know what?" I propped myself on my elbows and looked at Eric. "Leaving a message is a really good idea. But ... aliens? I mean, would people really buy the outer space thing? It seems kind of wacky. Heck, I'm only twelve and I wouldn't believe it."

Eric closed his eyes and sighed.

"If everyone in Sultana saw the same U.F.O., that would be believable," I said, trying to cheer him up. "But I don't think we can build a fake spaceship in the next three days. We'd need at least four."

Eric ignored my attempt to be funny, and we sat in silence again.

And then it hit me. "Wait!"

Eric's eyes popped open.

"What if we made a plaque or tablet with a message from some ancient civilization – you know, like the Aztecs, or Mayans or Egyptians – and then buried it? There's never been any evidence of those guys coming up here, so people will freak out if that's found in Sultana."

"Yeah ... that could work!" Eric jumped up and theatrically swept his arms over the valley. "They'll turn this whole area into a massive dig site. I can see it now, Cody. People scattered all over the place, digging like crazy, and finding nothing. Nothing but the fake stuff we bury for them." Eric laughed like an old vampire from a black-and-white movie. "Mwah, ha, haa."

I couldn't help but laugh too. "So what'll it be?" I asked when he finished giggling. "Mayan, or Aztec, or –?"

"– Rachel's got a book at home on Ancient Egypt. It has lots of pictures of tombs, and hieroglyphics, and that sort of stuff. We could start there and get some ideas."

"Excellent." I stood up and brushed off the dirt on my legs. I had to admit it was a crazy idea we had – maybe even a bit too crazy to pull off – but we had to try something. "Let's go. We've got to get this done fast to make it work."

CHAPTER 2

"Hey, Rachel!" Eric bellowed.

No answer.

The screen door slammed shut behind us and Eric yelled again. "Fivehead!"

I cringed at the nickname he had given his sister. Rachel's long hair was usually pulled back into a ponytail and that made it look like her forehead was bigger than normal. It wasn't really but one day when Eric was especially mad at her, he said her *fore*head was so big it was a *five*head. I know that makes no sense, but it was a nickname that stuck.

"We're lucky," Eric said, "she's not home."

We ran up the stairs, past Eric's room, and down the hall into Rachel's bedroom. Well, actually, I froze outside the doorway to her room and Eric went in and began the search for the book. It felt weird sneaking around someone's bedroom without permission.

Having never seen a girl's bedroom, I didn't know what I'd find, but it wasn't this. First of all, it was a mess. Not messy with clothes or dirt, but cluttered with stuff – neat stuff. Next to her dresser was a yellow milk crate filled with rocks, fossils, and what appeared to be bleached bones.

And the walls weren't pink. In fact, I couldn't tell what color they were. Two walls were plastered with movie posters, and two were painted floor to ceiling with a mural. The mural was a mountain landscape with castles, rivers, lakes, and dragons. Next to the window was a half-painted village she was still working on. A variety of brushes sat in a glass of dirty water on the window sill. And under the window was a tub with dozens of paint tubes and bottles.

And besides that, her bedroom was littered with books. Dozens of them ...

"What are you doing?"

I jumped at the sound of a voice behind me. It was Rachel. With all the noise Eric was making, I hadn't heard her come up. She was talking to her brother, but I felt my face heat up from guilt, or embarrassment, or something else.

Eric glanced up, but continued his search through a foot-high stack of hardcover books. "We need that book you have on Egyptians."

Rachel didn't look too upset. She stood next to me and watched Eric. Her suntanned forehead sparkled with tiny beads of sweat. She must have been running or biking. "Why?" Again, not mad –

just curious.

Eric didn't answer Rachel's question, so she said, "If you're not going to tell me why you want it, I won't give it to you. And you can leave my room *now*."

Eric stood up, frustrated. He scanned the room, and I knew he was thinking that we could just come back later. But by then Rachel might have stashed the book someplace where we'd never find it. We needed it right away.

I broke the tense silence. "Okay, we'll tell you," I said, "but you have to swear not to tell anyone."

Eric flopped into an old-fashioned barber chair in the center of the room and groaned. He clearly didn't want Rachel in on our hoax. "Cody, she's a girl," Eric whined.

"Yeah ..." I gave him a look like 'well, what do you suggest instead?', but he just rolled his eyes.

Rachel went into her bedroom and sat on the edge of the bed. "All right," she commanded, "let's have it."

I did most of the talking for the next ten minutes, though Eric interrupted twice to clarify. I had fun explaining to Rachel how our fake artifact was going to get everyone to come to Sultana – more fun than I expected. And how we'd be the kids who put our small town on the map. I left out the part about Rachel's mom getting fired from work, and the possibility they may have to move. She might not know yet, and I didn't want to be the one to tell her.

Rachel looked back and forth between the two of us, and finally said, "But *why*? I still don't see why it's so important to put Sultana in the spotlight."

I looked at Eric. No way was I going to answer that question.

Eric sighed. "A couple of days ago I heard Mom on the phone. She was saying that if business doesn't improve at the Rivercrest soon, and I mean real soon, she's going to lose her job. And that's bad enough, but if Mom can't work – you know what that means, right?"

Rachel responded with a frustrated shake of her head. I could tell, though, she was starting to get worried. I mean, if my parents lost their jobs, how would I feel about it?

Eric released an exasperated sigh and glanced away, staring intently at the unfinished mural. "If she can't work, we're gonna have to leave," he mumbled. "We're going to have to leave Sultana."

Rachel blinked a bunch of times – super fast. "Move away?" she said. "You mean, like forever?"

Eric nodded. "Unless we can get people to come to Sultana – and the Rivercrest."

Rachel took a long, deep breath. "Wow. I thought I'd never say this about this town. But I *really* don't

21

want to leave."

That was my cue again. "And you won't have to. We're not going to let that happen. Now you see why this hoax has to work?"

She looked at me and then at Eric. "Yeah. But how are you going to do it?"

I carefully explained the rest of our plan. And I relaxed a bit as I outlined it. From the looks of it, Rachel thought our idea was great – she kept nodding – but by the time I finished she was shaking her head.

Eric, who had been cranking the barber chair up and down all this time, stopped. "Why are you shaking your head?"

"Well, let me see if I have this right," she said. "You want to carve a message in ancient Egyptian hieroglyphics onto a tablet."

"Yeah," I said.

"Yup," Eric agreed.

"And then you want to hide this plaque so it'll be found by Dr. Murray."

We nodded some more.

She continued: "Dr. Murray will then take it to scientists who will be blown away by it and swarm the town."

"Yes!" Eric and I shouted.

Rachel scoffed and shook her head. "It won't work."

CHAPTER 3

"What do you mean it won't work?" Eric asked.

Rachel sighed. "Because any scientist with half a brain will figure out that it's a prank. And he'll do *that* in minutes."

"Why?" I asked.

"I'll show you why." Rachel left the bed, pushed around a bunch of CDs next to her dresser, and extracted a book from the debris. The title read *Egyptology For Everyone*.

She returned to the bed and placed the book on her lap, expertly flipping the pages to whatever section she wanted to show us. "Here it is," she announced. She set the book on the bed and pointed to a heading.

Eric left his chair to examine the book. "Check it out, Cody."

I dropped to my knees beside Eric and looked at the section Rachel was tapping with her finger. "'Egyptians In Australia'?" I read out loud. Beneath that was a smaller heading that said, 'Hoaxters in Gilmaroo Foiled'.

Eric and I read the entire page in silence, while

Rachel waited. It was about some pranksters who had attempted to reproduce hieroglyphic messages on the wall of a cave. But the inscriptions had been "immediately dismissed as a hoax."

A photo on the following page showed a dozen men standing around what looked like authentic Egyptian hieroglyphics. Some of the men – obviously the hoaxters – had big grins on their faces, while other men – perhaps the Egyptologists who had wasted time flying to Australia – looked extremely grouchy.

"Those carvings sure look real to me." I leaned in close for a better look.

"Yeah," Eric agreed, "they're pretty cool."

"But it's all gibberish," Rachel said. "The article goes on to say that the carvings are just a bunch of random symbols that don't mean anything. The pranksters probably just looked in a book about King Tut, and then copied a mix of drawings onto the cave. It looks impressive, but to an Egyptologist it reads like baby talk."

She twisted up her face, "The carvings probably said, 'Goo, goo, goo. Bla, bla, bla.'"

I laughed at her demo – even Eric chuckled a little, though he tried to hide it.

"But people would *still* have to come to Sultana to check it out," Eric jabbed the book with a finger. "Just like here in Australia."

"Not anymore," Rachel said. "That happened over fifteen years ago. If these same hieroglyphics were discovered today, someone would take a digital photograph, e-mail it to an expert – he'd laugh when he saw it – and then he'd call in the hoax. It would all happen within hours."

"And it might not even make the local paper," I said. "And we *need* to get the media's attention."

"Exactly," Rachel said, pleased we were catching on.

Eric jumped up and began pacing. I had my back to him now and felt kind of dumb kneeling on the floor, so I got off the carpet and sat on the bed.

"So the only mistake those guys in Australia made was not writing a real message," Eric said, winding his way around the clutter. "Right?"

"It seems like it," I agreed.

Rachel nodded.

"In other words," Eric continued, "if we inscribed a message that really meant something, it might fool people."

"At least for a while," I said.

"Hey!" Eric froze, suddenly excited. "Do you remember in French class, when we used that translator on the Internet to help us convert English words into French words? Well, maybe they have translators for hieroglyphics."

I wasn't so sure, but what if he was right?

"Yeah. It's worth a look."

Rachel bounced off the bed. "Well, then let's go to Cody's house."

"What? Why?"

"Because you have a computer." Rachel looked at me like I was the village idiot. Maybe I was.

Eric tried to shake his sister. "Don't you have to go next door and babysit Gwyneth?" Rachel often helped Mrs. Roberts watch her baby, Gwyneth, on mornings when she was working. Mrs. Roberts shared a rural mail route with some other lady from out of town.

"Nope. Not today." Rachel grinned fiendishly. "I have the *whole* day off."

Eric groaned and looked to me for support. He must have forgotten that we actually *needed* her help. I shrugged – he'd figure it out eventually.

CHAPTER 4

I knew Eric wasn't happy about Rachel tagging along, but he seemed to have gotten over it by the time we walked through the back door of my house.

"You got anything to drink?" he asked, opening the fridge before I could answer. It was 2:30 in the afternoon and Eric knew my mom was working at the park gate and wouldn't be home for hours.

Our desktop sat in the corner of the kitchen. We each grabbed a Coke and I pulled up three chairs, waiting for the computer to warm up. Since it was my house, I worked the keyboard, sandwiched between Rachel on my left and Eric on my right.

I clicked my way to an internet search engine. "Egyptian Translator?"

"Let's be even more specific," Rachel said. "How about 'Egyptian Hieroglyphic Translator'? Otherwise, we may get a modern translator."

Eric nodded, and I typed the words into the search box.

Three seconds later the screen filled with a list of websites that translated English words into ancient Egyptian hieroglyphics.

"Wow!" Rachel said. "That was too easy."

I went to the first site on the list and it asked me what I wanted translated.

"Try my name," Eric said eagerly.

I typed in E-R-I-C and pressed ENTER.

Eric was impressed. "How cool!" We were staring at a vulture, a mouth, a leaf, and a basket.

"Do mine now," Rachel said, moving closer.

R-A-C-H-E-L.

ENTER.

"Look," she said, in awe of the mystical symbols. Her index finger floated across the screen and touched each object lightly. "A mouth, an arm, a vulture ... hey, what's that one?"

I realized my mouth was so dry I couldn't talk. I quickly irrigated my tonsils with some Coke.

"I ... I think it's a TV," I mumbled without thinking.

"Don't be silly. They didn't have TVs in ancient Egypt."

"This will make it easy," Eric said. "All we have to do is enter our message, print out the translation, and carve it on our plaque. Then we'll have an authentic, mysterious Egyptian artifact." He leaned back in the chair, pleased.

We goofed around for the next hour, exploring the website and translating all sorts of names and words. M-O-M. D-O-G. F-I-V-E-H-E-A-D – that one got Eric a play-punch from Rachel – and so forth. Each time a new symbol popped up we would let out a "wow".

But then I stopped.

I'm not sure if it hit me first, or Rachel, but somewhere in our heads something clicked at the same time.

"Wait a minute!" I said. "Something's wrong."

"Yeah," she agreed. "This doesn't make any sense."

"What?" Eric grumbled. "What doesn't make sense?"

"The translator," Rachel said.

"Just look at the monitor." I jabbed at the screen with my finger.

Eric shook his head. "What are you guys talking about?" He ran his fingers through his blond hair. "You guys don't know Egyptian or hieroglyphics or whatever. How can you say it's wrong?"

Rachel leaned forward and touched the pictograms one at a time. "Look at these symbols for the last word that Cody entered. A rope, a vulture, a mouth, and so on. Right?"

"So? We've seen most of those symbols before in the other words."

"Yes," she said, "but Cody typed in *helicopter*."

"Don't you see?" I said. "They didn't have

helicopters in ancient Egypt."

"Shoot!" Eric leaned back in his chair. "So this translator only converts the *sounds* of our letters into Egyptian letters."

"Exactly," I said. "So if we made a plaque engraved with the symbols for 'King Tut was here', it would look impressive, but it would be in English."

"And be quickly dismissed as a hoax." Eric sounded depressed. "So we're at another dead end."

"Maybe not," Rachel said. "Could I try something?"

"Sure." I pushed the keyboard over to her.

Eric and I watched the computer, and tried to follow all the links she bounced to. After five minutes she found a website that made both Eric and me sit up – *Egyptian Pictographs* was the title.

We quickly read the first few pages. Rachel absorbed the information fast, while Eric and I barely kept up with the cursor as it scrolled down the page. The site was similar to the first one – it included all the basic symbols for the early Egyptian alphabet. But then it also explained how certain symbols and drawings – called pictograms – represented complete ideas or actions.

The web page had hundreds of drawings and next to each drawing was the English translation of what that pictogram meant.

"Look." Eric tapped the monitor with a dirty finger. I automatically wiped his fingerprint with my napkin. "They had symbols for almost everything."

They were organized on the website according to how frequently they had been used in ancient texts. Glyphs for man, woman, village, walking, and so on came first. And three pages later we found the lesser-used symbols. For example, there were over one hundred little drawings that represented the different parts of a ship.

"Wow!" I said. "Look at all the different scratchings they used for weapons." Now we were looking at pictograms for knives, shields, bows, and spears.

"Hieroglyphics must have included over a thousand symbols," Rachel marveled.

"We'll have to keep our message pretty simple," I warned.

"Yeah," Eric agreed. "If we try anything too complex or too wordy, it might not work."

I found a piece of paper and a pencil. "So ... what message should our ancient Egyptian explorers leave for the people of Manitoba?"

"Let's start with a date," Rachel suggested. "My book said they had dates based on the King that was ruling Egypt at the time."

"How the heck would that work?" Eric sounded grumpy again that Rachel had butted in on his great plan.

"It's *simple*, Eric." She wrinkled her nose, doing a really good impression of a snooty librarian. "Each time a new king started to rule, they would start at year one. So a date for our artifact might be 'the tenth year, fourth month, twentieth day, under the rule of King Tut'."

"Perfect," I said, taking notes. "Let's use that."

"But not the 'King Tut' part." Rachel shook her head. "That's too phony. Let's use some King no one's heard of. I can find one in my book later."

Eric nodded, grudgingly accepting that his sister was useful, smart, and here to stay.

"The hieroglyphics that the scribes used are pretty exact too," I said. "What if we start off by saying that the chief scribe on our expedition has died or been killed and that some student scribe is now doing the recording?"

"Yeah, that's good," Eric said. "Then if we really mess things up with the inscriptions, the experts will just think it was because some junior scribe took over. I love it."

Together we spent the rest of the afternoon debating a proper message that Egyptians may have left over three thousand years ago. At 4:30 we stopped and agreed what we had was perfect.

"Okay." I looked down at my final written copy. "Here's what I've got."

Twenty men died crossing water. Scribe is now with the gods of the Underworld. This foreign land is the enemy – harsh and cold. Ra has forsaken us. We have gone North on the wide river for too long. It now turns to ice under our bow. We have not the time to return. I fear I will not see my beloved Nile again. Osiris have mercy on our souls.

When I had finished reading it out loud, the three of us sat in silence. We could feel how weird it was. Almost like there really was an Egyptian who left that message for us thousands of year ago.

That's how good it sounded.

Until Rachel burst our bubble. "Now comes the hard part. Looking up those symbols and engraving them into something."

CHAPTER 5

"I'll print out these pages," I said, "and then work on the translations tonight after supper."

"We can get together again tomorrow morning," Rachel suggested, "and make the inscriptions."

Eric shook his head. "No. That won't work. Mom said I have to mow the lawn first thing in the morning. And that'll take an hour."

"So why can't Cody and I start on it?" Rachel glared at her brother.

Eric looked at me and then at Rachel. "Fine." He passed Rachel her backpack. "I'll see you around ten, Cody."

Rachel grinned and followed her brother to the door. "See you tomorrow. Is nine o'clock okay?"

I nodded my assent and walked them to the front door. I stared down the empty street for a while after they left, until I realized I still had loads of work to do. *Get it together, Cody.*

I returned to the computer and printed out every page that could possibly provide a useful pictogram. Our printer was painfully slow and I was worried Mom and Dad would be home before

I finished. Not because of all the paper I was using – well, that too – but because I didn't want them to see what I was printing. It wouldn't take them long to figure out who was behind an Egyptian hoax if they saw me staring at a website for hieroglyphics all night.

In fact, it was absolutely critical that no one become aware of our role in the fake plaque. If anyone were to catch us, at any point, it would be over – for all of us. I would be grounded for years. Well, maybe not years, but I'd be in major trouble. And when I finally did get to leave the house, I'd be all alone. ALL ALONE. Just the thought made me sick – seriously, it made me feel woozy. Who would I hang out with? Who would I ride the school bus with? Who would I go exploring with? I did *everything* with Eric.

And I couldn't imagine how awful it would be for Eric – having to move. Another town, another house, another school, and all without a single friend.

This plan had to work. Simple as that – no mistakes, no getting caught. We had to trick everyone and make people come to Sultana.

I had everything printed, the computer turned off, and was just putting the bundle of papers on the desk in my room when Mom and Dad came home. Dad barbequed hamburgers for supper – of which

I had three – while Mom did some accounting stuff on the computer. After dinner they went for their daily walk around Sultana, and I went to my bedroom and began looking up the right pictures for our message.

It was easier than I thought it would be. Several words were often represented by one or two symbols. For example, a scribe dying was so simple it was almost obvious. A 'scribe' was a drawing of a man in front of some sort of box thing – maybe a desk. And 'dying' was an outline of a person, all twisted-up, like a chalk outline at a murder scene. I think any Egyptologist would figure that out.

Each time I found the symbol I needed, I traced it onto a piece of paper.

Other pictograms were a bit harder to find, but turned out to be simple to draw. A 'foreign land' looked like two waves with a line under it. And 'to travel' was a pair of legs. I smiled as I traced the stickish figures.

The most difficult thing about doing the conversions to glyphs was trying to stay focused. My mind kept going back to Eric and his sister. The thought of them both leaving for good and never seeing them again made me feel like I had swallowed a pillow. Sure, I didn't want Eric to leave, but it would suck for Rachel too if she had to leave, and I didn't want that.

We had to make this work.

The next morning I woke up at eight to the grating chirp of my alarm. I never thought I'd ever use it during summer holidays, but I didn't want to look like an idiot when Rachel came over. Plus, getting this hoax together trumped everything else, even sleeping in.

I wolfed down a bowl of Cheerios by myself – Mom and Dad were already at work. It was still a bit early, so I waited on the couch where I could watch the road through the window. Except I could barely keep my eyes open. The kitchen clock chimed the hour and startled me awake. And then, on cue, the doorbell rang. I opened the door, rubbing my eyes. "Hi, Cody," she said, panting lightly. She definitely looked more awake than I did.

She shook off her pack in one fluid motion and set it on a chair. "Check it out." She extracted a writing pad. "Doesn't this look cool?" Rachel explained how she had copied pictograms for various dates from a page in her book, and then changed the dates by mixing the glyphs around.

I looked them over and nodded, recognizing

many of the curious shapes that represented numbers from the pages I had printed the night before. A lot of Rachel's glyphs were complicated profiles of people or birds, and she had captured the details perfectly.

I tapped the pad of paper where she had drawn three unfamiliar symbols closely together. "Are these for the king?"

"Yeah, that's him. His glyphs are a crane on a post, three feathers, and that shepherd's staff."

"What's his name?" I asked.

"Well, my book makes reference to a little-known King called Tuthmosis." She poked the three symbols in front of me. "And apparently, this Tuthmosis guy was kind of greedy, and was always searching for new trade routes."

"Excellent," I said. "So it would be logical – or at least possible – that Tuthmosis sent a bunch of explorers west across the ocean to find people to trade with."

"That's exactly what I thought. And I also made sure that the date of our exploration – and the plaque – falls within the reign of Tuthmosis."

"Huh?" I said.

Rachel laughed. "Well, we can't have the date on our tablet be a hundred years *before* King Tuthmosis was even born. That would give it away as a fake. As long as our explorers leave while the

King is ruling, it'll make sense."

Man, was she smart. "That's really good thinking," I said.

She blushed. "Well – what have you got?"

"What?" I asked.

"Your translations. Let's see them."

Sheepish, I showed her the hieroglyphics that I had traced the night before. She took the paper from me, sat down at the kitchen table, and began adding her glyphs to the top, so that everything would be on one page.

"This is going to be amazing once we engrave it onto a tablet." She put down the pencil and admired the page. "Very, very cool."

"How should we do the engraving?" I asked.

"Would it be too hard to carve into a stone?"

"I thought about that, but I think we'd just end up smashing it. If we had a huge stone, we could chisel the symbols into it – that's what they did in Australia – but it wouldn't work for a small plaque."

"What if we carved it into soft clay and then baked the clay in a fire or oven?" She pulled a banana from the fruit bowl in front of her and spun it like the *Wheel of Fortune*. "I think that's sort of the way the Egyptians did it."

I nodded. "That would work."

"But no one in Sultana does pottery, so we can't get any clay."

"I'm not positive," I said, "but I'm pretty sure my Aunt Dayna had once said that clay is clay – she's into ceramics and pottery stuff."

Rachel frowned. "What do you mean?"

"Well, pottery clay, is just clay. Right out of the ground. No additives, no nothing – it's clay. The same as the stuff found under the ground all over southern Manitoba."

She gave the banana another good spin. It skidded to the edge of the table but she grabbed it before it could fall onto the floor. "So we just have to find a deep hole and scoop some up."

"And I think I know where we can get some."

"Get some what?" Eric pushed open the screen door at the back of the kitchen. He barely looked at us before heading straight for the fridge.

I updated Eric about the clay for the tablet.

"Sure, that sounds good," Eric said, scanning the inside of our refrigerator. "How come you never have any chocolate milk?" He wiped his sweaty forehead on his shoulder.

"Jeez, Eric," Rachel scolded, "don't be so rude. This isn't your house."

I laughed. Rachel clearly hadn't seen Eric the way I had. "Take a glass of regular milk and just add some powder." I pointed to the pantry. "It's on the third shelf."

Eric closed the fridge door. "That's gross and

not the same at all."

Rachel shook her head. "Lazy."

Eric sat down with us at the table, and I told Rachel how we had once explored a construction site three kilometers west of Sultana. There, we found an enormous backhoe that had been busy excavating the foundation for a new dairy barn. It had been a Saturday and no one was working, so we explored the whole site without getting caught. There should be lots of clay there.

"Sounds like a perfect plan," Eric said, getting up. "Let's go now before it gets too hot out."

After tossing a few drinks in Rachel's backpack, we all rode past the Rivercrest and out of town on the gravel farming road.

There was rarely a vehicle on this stretch, so we pedaled side by side and didn't worry about traffic kicking up clouds of dust and choking us. The sun was already warm on our faces, the sky was cloudless, and I was beginning to believe our plan could work.

"There it is," I said, pointing at a rutted driveway that went on forever. We could see the backhoe but we didn't hear any heavy equipment, so we approached the yard without caution. I mean, even if someone was there, they would have just chased us away.

"It looks like we have the place to ourselves,"

Rachel said, leaning her bike against a pallet of plywood sheets.

"Maybe not." Eric walked over to the giant digger, put his hand on the motor cover, and quickly pulled it away. "This thing's been running today – it's still hot."

Rachel surveyed the area again. "We better hurry. They may come back any minute."

I agreed. We all knew the consequences of being caught removing clay from the construction site – the jig would be up, as they say.

Eric leaned his bike against a portable toilet. "Rachel's right," he said, pulling a cookie out of his pocket. "You guys get the clay, and I'll stand guard in case someone comes back."

Rachel shook her head. "He'll do anything to get out of doing the dirty work," she whispered.

"And where did he get those cookies?" I wondered out loud.

I took Rachel to the deepest part of the excavation. "I think this area here will be the dairy barn." I indicated an area surrounded with in-complete concrete forms. We jumped over the reinforced steel perimeter, and she followed me to the center, where an eight-foot-deep trench ran the length of the barn. "And this must be for some sort of cow manure collection system," I said.

Rachel nodded.

We had forgotten to bring a bag or container for storing the clay, so we prowled around the yard looking for something appropriate while Eric's eyes roved the horizon for surprise visitors.

"This will work," Rachel said, stooping over a pile of Styrofoam panels. She pulled a pocket-knife from her shorts, flicked open the largest blade, and cut a towel-sized piece of plastic wrapping from around the bundle.

I stared at her, impressed. She had to be the only girl I knew who carried a knife.

"I think we'll need this too." I yanked on a ladder that was weighing down a second pile of Styrofoam. The clay that had been removed from the trenches was spread out all over the site – but we wanted the fresh stuff from below.

"And that." She was looking at something over by a shed.

She hurdled over stacks of lumber and steel, and retrieved a shovel.

We returned to the trench and I lowered the ladder into the void. "Ladies first?" I asked, tossing the shovel in the pit.

Rachel rolled her eyes, but grabbed the top of the ladder without hesitating. "Thank you kindly. You are a true gentlemen." And with that, she disappeared down the rungs.

I followed her to the bottom. We made our

way along the cool trench. There was no water in the pit, but a damp, earthy smell engulfed us. Had I been alone, it may have creeped me out, but I felt comfortable with Rachel by my side. Well, actually, she was ahead of me. The trench was only three feet wide, so we couldn't walk side by side.

We stopped at a spot near the other end of the trench. Rachel crouched and ran her fingers across the face the earth on her right side.

"Feel this, Cody. It's so smooth, it's almost like glass or something."

It was hard to see clearly in the trench because the sun was still low on the horizon. I dropped the shovel and reached out, groping at the muddy wall.

"No." She moved my hand to the right. "Over here. Feel this."

"That's incredible," I muttered touching the earthen wall. "The damp clay down here has been smeared so smooth from the backhoe, it actually feels like pottery."

"Yeah," she whispered in awe. "It has to be pure clay."

I smiled – though in the dark Rachel probably couldn't see – and began to feel more confident that our scheme would work.

Or so I thought.

Rachel had just picked up the shovel to start digging when we heard a shout from above. It was Eric. "A TRUCK IS COMING!"

Startled, Rachel dropped the shovel on my foot. I was definitely not smiling anymore.

Ignoring the pain in my toe, I sprinted to the ladder and scurried up just enough to see what was happening. Eric was standing in the open, twenty feet away from the trench. And he was staring at a rapidly approaching cloud of dust.

Crap!

I jumped down into the pit again.

"He's not kidding," I warned. "There's a half-ton coming up the drive."

Rachel trembled. "What should we do? Should we all hide?"

"There's no point in Eric hiding – he's busted. If he tries to run now, he'll just look guilty. But we might as well stay down here and see what happens."

"What do you mean?" Rachel's eyes widened.

"It may only be some guy who needs directions," I said. "Let's just see what happens."

"And the bikes? If he sees our two bikes, he'll know something's going on. They could charge us for trespassing!"

I had totally forgotten about the bikes, but I was pretty sure they were hidden from view by another pallet of lumber. "I don't think they'll see them, as long as the person doesn't walk around."

I said a silent prayer to myself: *Please don't*

walk around.

The truck made more and more noise as the tires crunched against the spilled gravel near the work site. We waited anxiously for the vehicle to come to a stop. It seemed to take forever, but finally we heard the motor quit. Then a door opened and slammed shut.

"Only one person," I whispered, stating the obvious.

Rachel nodded. "I wonder what Eric's going to do?" She sounded calmer now.

Above us, we heard a man speak. "Hi," the voice said. "Is Peter around?"

After a lengthy pause, Eric replied, "No, he went to the restaurant for breakfast."

"What restaurant?" The man said – he sounded suspicious.

"The only restaurant." I groaned – don't be a smartass *now*, Eric! "The Rivercrest. It's over there. In Sultana."

I imagined Eric pointing toward town.

After another painful silence – a silence that made me really nervous – I heard the man say, "What are you doing here?"

"Uh oh!" Rachel groaned.

"I have diarrhea," Eric answered.

"What?" The man sounded like he was getting mad. I looked at Rachel – she didn't look like she had any idea what Eric was up to either.

"I had to use the port-a-potty."

This time I imagined Eric pointing at the construction site toilet.

"Well," the man said, "why didn't you just go home?"

"I was fishing over there, and I *was* going home, but then I had to go to the john. So I came here."

Silence.

"Do you want a ride home?" the man said.

"No thanks. I'm going fishing again, and anyway, I'm not supposed to take rides from strangers."

Rachel and I waited uneasily for a response from the man, but heard only silence. A few minutes later, the engine finally roared to life and we heard the truck drive away. And then –

"Man, was that a close call or what?" Eric said, grinning down at us from the ground above the trench. "I didn't think he'd ever leave."

I resisted the urge to go above ground and clobber him. He *had* just saved us with his quick thinking.

"We might as well forget about the clay and just leave right now." I reached for the ladder and began climbing. "It won't take him long to go to the Rivercrest and realize you lied." I gestured for him to move out of the way so I could lift myself out of the trench.

"I never lied," Eric said, stepping to the side. "Pete's at the Restaurant."

Rachel came up behind me. "Who the heck is Pete, anyway?"

"Don't you guys have any faith in me?" Eric pretended to be hurt. "Look." He pointed to the door on the backhoe.

Rachel and I turned. On the scratched door was a decal that said PETE'S BACKHOE SERVICE.

Eric continued, "And when we rode past the restaurant this morning, I noticed there was a dump truck in the parking lot that had the same sticker on the door. So I just put two and two together."

"You know, Eric," Rachel said, "that was pretty quick thinking."

"Yeah, I saved the day – just like Indiana Jones." Eric beamed with pride. "Now hurry up and get that stupid clay before someone else shows up. I'm all out of lame excuses, and cookies too." He wasn't lying. His cookies were gone except for the crumbs littered down his shirtfront.

Rachel didn't waste any time. She scampered down the ladder into the trench.

I turned to follow her, but before I got to the ladder I looked toward my bike. The handles were clearly visible, but the rest of the bikes were hidden. There was no way of knowing what our visitor had seen – or what he might report.

In the excavation trench again, Rachel and I took turns digging out and trimming a chunk of clay into a nice brick-sized piece. Then, we wrapped our prize in the plastic Rachel had found earlier, and headed back to Sultana.

CHAPTER 6

Eric picked up the cube of clay and tested its weight by bouncing it lightly in his hand, like a pitcher about to throw a baseball. "So now what?" He said. "Should we cut off a slab and start engraving?"

This was actually a good question, because we'd never talked about how we would make the plaque.

I sat down next to Rachel by the picnic table in Eric and Rachel's backyard. "Egyptians carved hieroglyphics onto the tombs by smearing the stone walls with clay or mortar first," I said. "Then they engraved the soft clay before it hardened. Couldn't we do that too?"

Eric collapsed on the lawn. He was either tired of cutting grass all morning, or he sensed another complication.

"I'm sure we could do that." Rachel stretched her legs out in front of her. "We can take a rock, smooth a layer of clay onto it, and then carve the message."

"That would also make our plaque more solid," I added. "Because who knows how hard our clay alone will be."

Eric sighed and said, "Yeah, but all the rocks

around here are pure granite. It's almost impossible to find a thin piece in Sultana – granite's too much like a boulder. We could search for months and not find a good piece."

"You know what would be cool?" I said. "If we had some kind of rock that couldn't even be found in Manitoba – or at least not around here – and then wrote our message on that."

Rachel wiped her forehead. "Yeah, that'll really give the experts something to ponder. Archaeologists and Egyptologists would assume that our explorers picked up the rocks on their travels through North America."

Eric jumped up without warning. "You guys stay right here. I think I have just the thing."

Rachel and I didn't even have a chance to respond. In a second, we were watching him disappear inside the house.

Five minutes later he reappeared and handed me a grey piece of cardboard. Only it wasn't cardboard. It was a rock – a rock the size of a license plate, and not much thicker. "Where did this come from?" I asked, nodding at the thin slab as I turned it over and over.

"It's slate," Eric said, grinning.

"Slate?" I echoed.

"Yeah. A roofing slate. They used them in the old days instead of wooden shingles, so that if sparks came out of the chimneys –"

"– The houses wouldn't burn down. I get it," I said. "But where did *you* get it?"

"Our Uncle Oliver brought it back as a souvenir from someplace down in the United States – maybe New Orleans. It's been in our basement on a shelf for years."

"And Mom will never miss it," Rachel added. "Not that she even remembers we have it. If our explorers came up the Mississippi – like we're making it appear – they would've paddled past tons of slate deposits on the way here. It's perfect."

I continued staring at the stone in my hands. It really was ideal. Egyptians *wouldn't* have traveled across the ocean with heavy stone tablets, but once they got here, if they wanted to record their adventures, the slate would have provided the ultimate backing for their hieroglyphic records.

I felt more optimistic than ever that we could pull off our prank. I stood and passed the stone slab to Eric.

"Then let's go make us an artifact." Eric snatched the tablet from me and held it up over his head. "Because that's what Indie would do."

Rachel shook her head and laughed. "Somehow ... I can't see Indiana Jones making a fake artifact."

After Rachel rewrapped the clay, the three of us pedaled back to my house. The best place to work was the garage: Dad kept a great workbench and lots of little hand tools there.

"How do we slice this?" Rachel asked. She thumped the clay down onto Dad's countertop, next to the slab of rock.

Eric scrutinized the pegboard on the wall. "Saws are for cutting." He grabbed a handsaw that was hanging next to a collection of wrenches, hammers, and pliers. "And your dad has enough of them."

Rachel and I watched as Eric tried to cut through the clay like he was sawing a stick in half. Only the clay wouldn't cut. The teeth gummed up after his first stroke, and that was it. No more cutting.

"Try pushing down on the blade," Rachel said, "without sawing."

Eric lined up the saw again, and put all his weight on it.

Nothing!

Our brick of raw clay now had a dent in it, but not a clean cut.

"This is stupid," Eric complained. He hung the muddy saw on the wall again.

I made a mental note to clean it before Dad

noticed all the clay on it. "We need something super thin and super sharp," I said, looking around.

"CHEESE!" Rachel cried suddenly.

Eric and I both jumped.

"Huh?" I said.

"On TV, when they're cutting a huge brick of cheese, they use wire. Cheese is kind of like that clay. Right?"

"Absolutely." I quickly rummaged through the boxes under the bench. I found what I was looking for after a few minutes. It was a coil of thin copper wire, which Eric and I had used the year before to fashion animal snares. We had dreamed of making money selling furs, but couldn't bring ourselves to do it. We let the first rabbit we snared go free and dismantled our trap line the same day.

I uncoiled two feet of wire and wound each end around a screwdriver. "Here we go." I stretched the wire by yanking on the screwdrivers and pushed down on the brick of clay.

"Perfect," Rachel said, clapping her hands together with unabashed delight.

Eric cradled the first slice of clay in his hands, placed it on the shingle, and then attempted to fake a British accent. "Please, sir, may I have another piece."

We all laughed. And like a butcher in a meat

shop, I cleaved off another half-inch thick slice.

Rachel placed that piece next to the first. "We'll need one more," she said.

I cut a third slice, positioned it on the slate, and trimmed away the excess with my wire knife. Rachel, who had a softer touch, pressed the clay against the stone. The stone had a smooth, almost slippery feel to it, which made me nervous, but Rachel got the clay to bond firmly with the rock.

"Yeah." Eric leaned in close, with his elbows on the workbench. "That's perfect."

"Cody, go get some water," Rachel said without looking up.

"But I'm not thirsty ..."

"– For the clay, Cody. If I had some water, I could work out these seams." Her fingers ran down one of the lines where the clay pieces butted together.

"Right." I left before she could see the foolish look on my face. I took an old ice cream container outside, and brought back some water from a rain barrel.

Rachel dipped her fingers in the water and continued rubbing the surface. She was doing such a great job, Eric and I didn't bother offering to take over.

"How's this?" Rachel leaned the plaque against the pail of water and wiped her face with the back of her wrist.

She had pressed the clay perfectly into the slate, the seams had disappeared, and the whole surface was smooth and shiny.

"This is going to work," Eric whispered, more to himself than to us. "I just know it."

I unfolded the message I had drafted last night and placed it next to the unfinished tablet. "Then let's start carving," I said.

Rachel pleaded with us to be allowed to do the inscriptions onto the clay, and after seeing her bedroom art, I had no doubt she would do the best job. She pulled an old bar stool up to the workbench while I searched for pointy tools that she could use.

I sent Eric to the house to find some cookies and drinks – we hadn't had any lunch yet and I was getting hungry.

I sliced another wedge off the original brick for Rachel to experiment on. She selected a tool and practiced carving the pictogram symbolizing death. She was trying to use a flat-head screwdriver like a pencil to press and cut the image into the clay, but the edge kept digging in, making it tough to carve smoothly.

"Hold on, Rachel ... I got an idea."

I took the screwdriver from her and started up the electric grinder at the other end of the workbench. When it had finished vibrating up to speed, I ground the tip of the tool so that one of the flat sides no longer had a blunt edge.

Rachel dipped the head in the pail of water, and leaned over the practice slab again. With the new edge on the screwdriver, and the water acting as a lubricant, she effortlessly cut a symbol into the surface. The symbol looked unfamiliar and wasn't on my notes.

"What's that one mean?" I asked.

"It's one I found in my book." She started on a new glyph. "It means 'friendship'."

"Oh," I said. "It's, uh, nice."

"What's nice?" Eric asked, returning to the garage with granola bars, apples, cookies, and drinks. He dumped a week's supply of food – food from our kitchen, if I may add – on the workbench, while Rachel showed him a sample of her handiwork.

Eric nodded vigorously, and in between bites of his granola bar, said, "Great, Rachel. Work on the real one now. Forget the practicing. Cody's mom is going to be home soon."

My head automatically turned to look at the old kitchen clock on the wall. "Yikes!" I said. "We've got maybe an hour before she'll be here."

Rachel ordered us to back off and got ready to work on the real thing. I hung a utility light over her head and she spent forever adjusting it to reduce the glare. Finally, she took a deep breath, bent over the slab, and, like a surgeon, prepared for the first cut.

"Wait!" Eric screamed in alarm.

Rachel leaned back and gave a frustrated sigh. "What?"

"Remember what that book of yours said? Egyptian hieroglyphics were usually written from right to left, not like English."

"Good point." Rachel exhaled deeply, blowing strands of hair away from her face. "That could have been a major mistake. I'll have to reverse the order of Cody's pictograms here on his page."

She studied my first glyph again, took another breath, and began carving the top right corner of the plaque.

Eric and I paced the garage, ate cookies, and paced some more. Every five minutes – to Rachel's annoyance, I'm sure – one of us would stick our head over the work bench to see how much she'd done. She would look up and frown, and we'd shrink away again, feeling like scolded puppies.

The waiting really *is* the hardest part.

Eric, meanwhile, discovered an old *Tarzan* comic book and made himself comfortable in a lawn chair. A pile of food rested precariously on his stomach.

I couldn't relax, though. I wanted Rachel to work as fast as she could, before Mom got home.

But I also wanted the tablet to be perfect, so I had to let Rachel work at her own pace.

I tried to kill time by pretending to clean and organize the area around Rachel. I hung up tools on the pegboard, moved boxes around, and even swept the floor. I kept an eye on her progress and the driveway, watching for Mom's car. I was sure I was irritating her, but she was either too polite to yell at me, or so engrossed with her work she didn't care.

Thirty minutes later, she finally stopped.

I wondered if she had had enough of me and was going to kick me out of the garage. Standing two feet from her, I had been spending a ludicrous amount of time sorting Dad's collection of pliers. I got ready to explain how my dad liked all his tools sorted according to size, or color, or ...

Rachel groaned.

Eric looked up, but remained in his lawn chair. "What's wrong?"

"Nothing." She shrugged her shoulders in circles. "I'm just getting muscle cramps."

"Do you want me to finish it?" I moved closer to get a glimpse of her handiwork.

"Thanks. But I think for consistency, I better do it."

She reached over her head and massaged her back.

That was when I looked over her shoulder.

"Holy smokes," I said, seeing the half-finished plaque. "That's amazing. You gotta look at this, Eric."

He grunted, but refused to budge from his seat. He had obviously decided that if there wasn't a problem, then he wasn't on call.

Rachel beamed as she picked up the plaque and handed it to me. I ran my fingers along a few of the symbols. Each pictogram was carved to the same depth, and had crisp clean lines – it was flawless. "Gosh are we lucky you're doing this. Eric and I would've messed it up for sure."

Rachel's face reddened from the compliment, but then she looked over at her brother. She grimaced and I got the sense she knew I was right.

I stayed at her side as she resumed engraving. After every glyph she would pause and display it to me for approval.

Each time I would mutter something – "nice," "stylish," "too cluttered," and so on.

Once when she showed me a pictogram of a river, I shook my head sadly, and told her that she had inserted the wrong symbol.

Rachel's head snapped back to my notes. Two seconds later, she realized I was joking and jabbed me in the ribs. "That's not nice," she said, laughing. "I believed you."

"SHHH!" Eric hissed suddenly. "I think I hear a car."

Shoot! I'd totally lost track of time. Jumping over some boxes, I raced to look out the small door at the side of the garage. "It's my mom!" I announced.

Rachel froze at the workbench.

Eric dropped his comic on the floor and bolted to the window. "Now what?" He squinted through the dirty pane. "Will she come in here?"

I thought for a moment. Mom and Dad never parked the car in the garage – it was more like a big storage shed. "We should be okay." I looked around the cluttered space. "Unless she needs something, she won't bother us."

I prayed she didn't need anything.

Rachel didn't look convinced. "Maybe I should stop. We can finish it tomorrow."

Eric spun around and faced his sister. "No. Just finish it. We don't have enough time. You're almost done anyway."

Rachel looked down at the tablet and then up at me.

I nodded – it was a risk worth taking. "Yeah, let's get it done. Eric and I will stand guard and make sure she stays in the house."

Without another word, Rachel turned to the workbench and continued working on the clay tablet.

Then, ten minutes later, I heard the worst sound I could imagine – the familiar bang of the screen door by the side of the house.

Three seconds later my mom came around the corner carrying something.

I didn't even think – I just reacted.

As casually as I could, I walked out of the garage toward my rapidly approaching mom. Twenty feet from the door I pretended to notice her for the first time. "Oh, hi, Mom."

"Hi, Cody," she said. "What are you up to?" She wasn't suspicious – that's what she always asked when she saw me.

"Oh, nothing." I was trying really hard to control the panic in my voice. I reached for the garbage bag she was carrying. "I can put that in the garage for you," I offered.

She probably thought this was silly since she had lugged the bag ninety percent of the way already. She gave me a quizzical look, but passed me the garbage anyway. She didn't say anything though, just said thanks and turned to go back to the house. My heart didn't stop pounding until I saw her disappear around the corner. Then I sighed with relief.

That was way too close!

Three minutes later, I was standing next to the workbench again. Eric kept watch at the window and Rachel finished the message by adding the date to the very top of the plaque. Then she surprised me again. Rachel took her carving tool and etched a box around the three symbols that represented King Tuthmosis.

"Why'd you do that?" I asked.

"When ancient hieroglyphics mentioned any King," Rachel explained, "they always encircled the name, making it a cartouche. Out of respect, I guess. Anyway, there it is. All done."

CHAPTER 7

"How are we going to bake it?"

"What?" Rachel glared at Eric. She sounded offended by the idea of cooking her masterpiece.

We had taken the tablet from the garage and shuttled it to Rachel and Eric's backyard. There, under a shady Elm tree, we pondered our next move.

"Well, we can't just leave it in the sun to dry." Eric wiped a speck of chocolate from his mouth. "That'll take too long. We have to heat it up, so that it gets good and hard."

"Could we make a fire?" Rachel asked. "And bake it on the coals? That's probably what the Egyptians would have done anyway."

"Not this year," I said. "The campfire bans are already in place, to prevent forest fires."

"What about just sticking it in the oven?" Eric offered. "It might stink up the house a bit, but our mom won't be home for hours."

It made sense. There was no point in taking the plaque back to my house, since my mom was home now and we'd just narrowly escaped getting caught by her.

"Good idea," I said. "Let's go cook up a piece of history."

The oven seemed to take forever to heat up, and I was watching the kitchen clock as much as the oven window. Eric cranked the heat to maximum – probably over 450 degrees Fahrenheit – and Rachel slid the plaque in the stove on top of a piece of aluminum foil. All three of us sat around the oven, and one of us periodically leaned forward to see if anything was happening.

Every muscle in my body tensed as the minutes went by. First I was worried that the plaque would blow up and destroy the stove. Then, I fretted that our masterpiece would crack, crumble and disintegrate – all in front of our eyes. And as if that wasn't bad enough, I thought I could smell burnt mud.

"I smell smoke," Eric said.

"Me too," Rachel confirmed.

We watched in horror as grey smoke drifted from the front of the oven, near the top of the door, and spilled into the room.

Eric jumped up and opened the kitchen door before the smoke alarm could go off.

"Should we turn the oven off?" I wondered.

Eric sniffed the air. "It's not too bad yet. Let it

finish cooking."

Ten minutes later, Rachel leaned forward and squinted through the tiny oven window for the hundredth time. "Something's happening. Quick! Take a look!"

Eric and I dove off our chairs, wedged our heads next to Rachel's, and peered through the glass. She was right. Through the smoke we could see that the clay no longer looked shiny – it was drying. And hair-like cracks were spreading out across the surface. I didn't think this was bad as long as all those small cracks didn't form huge cracks – because then it would be unreadable.

Rachel got up and went upstairs to open more windows.

I turned to Eric. He was staring at the clay with an anxious look. "Don't worry," I said. "It'll only look better if it's cracked up a bit."

He didn't look convinced. "Gosh, I hope this works," he mumbled. Eric paced the room in a quick circle and looked through the glass again.

"It'll work." I tried to sound confident. "We just have to continue to be careful, and we can't get caught."

Another five slow minutes passed without any explosions or major cracks. Eric and I agreed that the plaque was likely as dry as it would get, so he turned off the oven and left the door open. Smoke poured out as Eric carefully extracted the slab with a protective oven mitt. He placed the tablet on the open door, and fanned the smoke away so that we could inspect it.

"MOM'S COMING HOME!" Rachel screamed from the second floor. Three seconds later, she was racing down the stairs. "Oh my God, the kitchen is full of smoke!"

"How can she be home now?" Eric asked. He didn't sound panicked at all. "It's only four."

Rachel ignored him. "I was opening my bedroom window when I saw Mom down the street. She's talking to Mrs. Klock."

Eric wrapped the plaque in a beach towel and put it in his sister's backpack. "She must have started at six today instead of eight."

"I think we're busted." Rachel fanned the air with a tea towel. "It stinks in here."

"No, no, no," Eric said, pacing the room. "We can't give up now."

"He's right," I said. "The tablet is baked. It's done."

Rachel continued to swing the towel frantically. "But what about all the smoke? She's going to be here in five minutes. She's going to know we were up to something."

"Listen." I turned to Rachel. "Go upstairs as quick as you can and paint anything – anything at all. Do it as fast as you can."

"Why?"

"We'll shove it back in the oven, and you can tell your mom you just wanted it to dry fast."

Eric nodded vigorously. "Do it, Rachel! Hurry! Cody and I'll clean up down here."

Rachel bolted up the stairs as we desperately tried to ventilate the kitchen the best we could. Mrs. Klock was known to babble and babble and babble, so if we were lucky she may stall Eric's mom long enough for Rachel to paint something and throw it in the oven.

It was going to be close!

We had escaped getting caught at the excavation, avoided getting trapped by my mom, now we just had to get lucky a third time.

What a day!

Eric flipped the oven back to max just as Rachel rushed into the kitchen.

She was holding something in a paint-splattered piece of newspaper – I couldn't see what – and she dumped it on a fresh piece of aluminum foil just as we heard the front door open.

I closed the oven door as quickly and quietly as I could. Then I moved to the left of the oven and crossed my arms, trying to look casual.

We didn't hear anything for about five seconds and then –

"Rachel! Eric! What's that smell?" To my relief, Mrs. Summers didn't sound mad.

Not yet, anyway.

"Oh, hi, Mom," Rachel called out. I was impressed by how innocent she sounded. "We're in here."

Mrs. Summers walked into the kitchen and let out a loud, "Phooey! *What* on earth are you kids cooking?"

Eric's voice was low when he spoke. He was probably trying to hide his guilt too. "Sorry about the smoke, Mom. We're just in a hurry to dry something."

"What is it? It sure stinks."

Eric and I opened our mouths, but since we didn't know *what* Rachel had painted, we closed them again.

She jumped in and saved us, "Look, we'll show you." Rachel opened the door and we all saw three freshly painted arrowheads – a yellow one, a red one, and a blue one.

"Hmmm." Mrs. Summers shook her head. "I don't know why you couldn't let them dry outside."

"No." Eric shook his head. "The paint sticks better if it's baked under extreme heat." He said that like it was super-obvious, which I thought was kind of funny.

"I think it survived," Eric said, his nose inches from the still-warm clay surface. "There are only a few cracks here and there." He stood up. "All right, let's go bury it."

But Rachel and I just sat there, at the picnic table, staring at the tablet. We were well away from the house, and hidden from sight of any neighbors' windows. Something about the tablet didn't look right and Rachel knew it too. The two of us had had the same thought again.

"It's too crisp," she said, resting her chin on her fist and studying the plaque.

"Yeah," I agreed. "It's too edgy."

Eric groaned. "Crisp? Edgy? What're you guys talking about?"

"Well, look at the thing," I said. "It doesn't look a thousand years old. Heck, it doesn't look a week old."

Eric moaned and sat down again.

"Cody's right," Rachel said. "It's not weathered, or worn, or anything. Each pictogram still has the same clean edge it had three hours ago. We have to deteriorate this plaque three thousand years."

"What if we stick it in your dishwasher?" Eric suggested.

I shook my head. "No way!"

Rachel's forehead creased, deep in thought. "What about putting it in a washing machine?"

"Hmmm," I pondered. "That may work. But the water might dissolve all the clay."

"Or worse," Eric said. "It might get all smashed up in there."

"So we need to wear it down," Rachel said, "without getting it wet."

"Yeah ..." I snapped my fingers. "And I know just the place to do it."

Rachel stayed with the tablet while Eric and I raced back to my place. He helped me look for something in the garage – something that I knew we would need. Then with our objects at the ready, the three of us walked across the street to Mr. Jelfs' shop.

Mr. Jelfs was a retired mechanic who now spent his spare time restoring classic cars. He had every tool in the world in his huge shop, and often helped fix Dad's lawnmower or weld something on my bike.

Mr. Jelfs was always teasing me, and I know he liked it when I bugged him back. I was never disrespectful – that would be going too far – but he told me he liked a kid with 'spirit' and that he enjoyed a good laugh. In fact, he was usually pretty grumpy *until* I played a prank on him. Mr. Jelfs would be suspicious if I wasn't slightly cheeky when we showed up. I had to come up with something silly, or he might just kick us out of his shop for 'loitering' as he put it.

But I was nervous and had trouble concentrating. It wasn't until we got to his garage that I thought of a good one.

I turned to Rachel and quickly explained how Mr. Jelfs appreciated a kid – or anyone really – who knew something about cars. "So make sure you tell him that you like that *Chevette* he's working on."

"Why?" she asked. Eric gave me a curious look too, but kept his mouth shut.

"Well," I said. "He's kind of grouchy and we need to get on his good side A.S.A.P. – so we can use his tools."

Just then we heard a crash inside the shop, followed by the sound of Mr. Jelfs cursing.

"See," I said. "He's already having a bad day."

Rachel suddenly looked nervous. "Okay. I'll try and go along with it."

The big double doors on his shop were open, and we could see him rubbing his head under the hood of his latest project. I think he'd just bashed his noggin. Mr. Jelfs heard us approach, gave the chrome air filter a final wipe, and turned to face us. His eyes surveyed us, looking for the busted objects we wanted fixed today. Seeing nothing, he relaxed.

I gave him a formal nod, same one I always did, and said, "Hi, Mr. Jelfs."

He nodded back. That was his customary way of granting me permission to enter his shop.

We stopped when we got to the car. I turned to Rachel and nodded. She looked so nervous I had to work hard to keep from smiling. I pretended to rub my cheek against the sleeve of my shirt.

"I like the color of this *Chevette*, Mr. Jelfs," she said.

He looked from Rachel to me, and back to Rachel again. "Did Cody here put you up to this?"

When he saw Rachel's confused face, Mr. Jelfs shook his head, laughed, and slapped me on the back. "This is a *Chevelle*, Rachel. A 1966 *Chevelle*. And Cody knows it too. There's a huge difference between a *Chevelle* and a *Chevette*."

Eric chuckled. Rachel's cheeks and the tops of her ears turned a bright shade of pink.

"Well," she said calmly, "they do sound the same."

Mr. Jelfs face creased up some more and he shook his head again. "Oh, sure, they may sound similar, but they're nothing alike. A *Chevelle* is a cool muscle car with style." He affectionately wiped a microscopic stain from the fender. "While a *Chevette* ... Well, let's just say that's a car everyone wants to forget."

I felt relieved. Rachel hadn't meant to, but she had gotten the job done.

The conversation turned to some polite small talk. Mr. Jelfs asked after my parents and talked at length about the weather. I could tell Eric and Rachel were getting antsy, and I was too. Finally, when I heard him pause, I said, "Could we use your sand blaster for a minute, Mr. Jelfs?"

"What for?" He looked behind us again, toward the door of the shop – probably thinking we had a pile of junk littering his driveway outside.

I pulled an old Howitzer shell casing from Rachel's pack and showed it to him. "We want to shine this up."

He took the foot-long brass shell from me and examined it carefully. "Where'd you find this?"

"I bought it at a garage sale for a buck," I said, telling the truth. I thought it was pretty cool when I first bought it, but by the time I got it home, I didn't know what to do with it so I tossed it in the garage.

Mr. Jelfs returned the oversized bullet. "You know what?" He gently rubbed his head where he banged it. "You could've polished this in the time it took you to get over here." He mumbled a bit more about how lazy kids were and then said, "Go ahead. But don't waste all my sand."

We thanked him and headed for the sand

blasting box sitting in the far corner of the eight-car garage. The unit looked like a small coffin with a window on the top and on the sides. Any object you wanted cleaned or ground down was placed in the box and sprayed with sand using compressed air. He had let me use it in the spring when I found an old bicycle frame at the dump. I wanted to repaint it, and used the sand blaster to clean away the rust. It had taken only minutes to strip it to bare metal.

I pretended to check the sand hopper while we waited for Mr. Jelfs to get back to his Chevette – I mean, Chevelle. When we were sure he was distracted, I switched the shell casing with the plaque, and shoved it through the opening. I closed the window, put on thick protective gloves, and started the compressor.

With my arms in the box, I picked up the sand sprayer and gently squeezed the trigger.

PSSSSSSSS

Sand shot out of the gun, startling all three of us. I knew it wouldn't take much to disintegrate the whole plaque, so I held the nozzle two feet away and gave the trigger a quick squeeze. A fine stream of sand shot out and instantly weathered the bottom corner. The sharp edges disappeared, giving the corner a tired, ancient look.

I held it up to the window for Eric and Rachel

to see, and they both nodded their approval above the din of the compressor.

Using the same technique, I hit the whole surface with another three-second burst of sand. Perfect. Then when I turned the plaque over to shake off the sand, I thought, what the heck, and gave the slate backing a shot of sand too.

As soon as I pulled it from the box, Eric flicked off the compressor, and Rachel stashed the tablet away in her pack. What a team!

We had almost escaped the garage when we heard Mr. Jelfs behind us.

"So?" He stared at us with his hands on his hips. "How'd it turn out? Let's have a look."

Busted!

Since I was in charge, I felt I should answer, but all I could come up with was, "Uhhhh ..."

"We decided we want to paint it instead, Mr. Jelfs," Rachel said, evenly. "So there's no need to waste your sand. But thanks."

Mr. Jelfs had a look on his face that said it all. As far as he was concerned, the three of us had just bumped several people off of Sultana's village idiot list. We left him shaking his head as we marched across the street to Eric and Rachel's house.

Out of sight of nosy neighbors, Rachel placed the plaque on the picnic table and we had a good look at it. Nothing about the slab looked fresh, or new, or crisp anymore – it looked a thousand years old. Even the glyphs had been altered, their edges and corners worn in different ways.

It looked ancient.

"This couldn't possibly look more authentic," Eric said, blowing some fine sand from the pictograms. "So *pulleeez* tell me we can go plant this once and for all."

I coughed from the dust he blew in my face. "Yeah, it's ready."

Rachel clapped her hands and beamed.

CHAPTER 8

The next morning we pedaled across town and up the road to our hideout above the MacFie River. On the way there, I explained to Rachel our plan for having the tablet discovered and revealed to the world.

She didn't seem impressed.

"Let me get this straight," Rachel said, easily keeping pace with Eric and me. "We're going to stick this in the mud, somewhere near the dock, and Dr. Murray's *accidentally* going to find it while he's fishing?"

Eric threw his head back and let out a whoop. "That's right, sis. You just wait and see."

Once at the hideout, we parked our bikes and scanned the river carefully, to make sure Dr. Murray hadn't returned for some reason.

He hadn't, and no one else was in sight either.

"You see," I said to Rachel, settling down under my favorite wedge of shade, "Dr. Murray fishes from the dock most mornings until he's caught his limit –"

"How do you know that?" Rachel interrupted.

She pulled out the plaque and gave it to Eric, who had been lurking around her backpack with his hands open.

Eric sat on the ground and began running his fingers over the glyphs. "Because," he said, "that's what he did all last summer. And it looks like he's going to do it this summer."

Rachel seemed satisfied with that part of the problem. "But where are we going to put it?" She pushed a stray lock of gold hair out of her face, and flopped down next to her brother and across from me.

Eric and I laughed because that was what made Dr. Murray the *perfect* discoverer.

"Dr. Murray has a certain style of fishing," I explained. "When he casts his line, he always – and I mean *always* – throws the lure right across the river to the far bank. And then he begins reeling it in toward the dock."

Rachel squinted across the MacFie. "But the river's low and there's a huge washout on the other side."

"Exactly," Eric said, "we stick this sucker in the mud, just at the water's edge –"

"– And wait for Dr. Murray to see it when he's fishing," Rachel said, cutting him off. "Okay, I suppose that makes sense. I just hope he's got good eyes."

79

"Oh, he's got good eyes," I said. "I mean, he doesn't wear glasses for fishing, anyway. And he always seems to throw that hook within three feet of the far bank."

Eric cleared his throat and continued to play with Rachel's handiwork. "We want people to take this seriously," he said. "Right?"

Rachel and I nodded.

Eric continued, "And it would be cool if people came and dug around a bit. Right?"

Again, our heads bobbed.

"And it would be good –"

"– For Pete's sake," Rachel said. "Just spit it out."

Eric paused. "Well, what if we chip off a corner of this plaque – only a small piece – and then bury that too?"

I sucked in a deep breath, expecting Rachel to throttle her brother. The nerve of the guy, wanting to break her beautiful ...

"Okay," she said.

"Huh?" I was stunned. Did the heat finally get to her? A mist of sweat was forming on Rachel's face again.

"We can snap off a section of the date, near the top corner." She reached out and tapped the clay. "And then bury the smaller piece in the washout – somewhere higher up in the bank."

I began to see the light too, and grabbed the plaque from Eric. "It would also appear logical," I said, "that the message – I mean, the tablet – somehow broke when it was bashed around over the centuries."

Eric and I were debating which one of us should break the slab when Rachel snatched the plaque from me and lined up the top corner with a sharp boulder. I held my breath.

CRAAACK.

The hit was clean, and left a single smaller piece lying on the ground. She picked up the fragment and examined the glyph.

She smiled and said, "Tuthmosis."

Eric took the tablet from Rachel, spit on it, and carefully ground the sharp edges of the fresh break against a rock.

Rachel took her piece and began rubbing her chunk against the granite surface too. "Good thinking, Eric."

Eric started laughing.

"What's so funny."

"I think this is called 'making history'."

We all agreed that we were at a critical stage in our hoax, and that from this point on we had to be extra, *extra* cautious. For the plan to succeed, it was important that no one see us near the burial site from either the dock or the bridge. It would be a shame if the plaque was discovered and someone said, "Hey, I saw Cody, Eric, and Rachel digging down there the day before."

Anyway, after winding our way back through the forest, we hit the highway and crossed the bridge. There, we hid our bikes in the bush and finalized our plan. We decided that Rachel would stay with the bikes, near the bridge and the highway. I would make my way along the bush line until I was above the eroded area. Eric would stay halfway between Rachel and me, and pass on any warnings that Rachel called out to him.

Rachel gave me the plaque and the fragment. Scared I'd lose the small chunk, I quickly slipped it in my pocket.

"And remember," she said, "don't go down to the waterline until you hear the signal."

"Piece of cake," I said, following Eric into the bush. "I got the easy job."

Man, was I wrong about that.

Eric and I battled our way through thick willows and black flies for five minutes. Then we headed west toward the bank of the MacFie. Walking got better when we hit the forest and the big trees. I could see the river through the branches now, so we paused to catch our breath.

Eric cupped his hands and yelled, "RACHEL. CAN YOU HEAR ME?"

Three seconds went by, and then we heard, "LOUD AND CLEAR."

"Good," Eric said, studying the other side of the river. "I can hear Rachel, and I can see the bridge and the washout from here."

"Okay, I'll stay out of sight, up top. Then if the coast is clear, I'll dash down to the river and stick the plaque in the mud."

"Sounds like a plan." Eric scratched his back against the trunk of a spruce tree. "And remember to keep the side with the hieroglyphics facing the dock."

I snuck along the upper edge of the bank for another three hundred feet until I was facing the clearing above the washout. From up close, it looked like a natural depression had drained the area for centuries, but somehow the sloping ground got saturated and overwhelmed by too much meltwater at one time. With an unstable river bank below, the wall of earth had caved into the MacFie, taking tons of rock and soil along for the ride.

But enough with the geography lesson.

I crouched and examined the edge of the river. Estimating that it would take me fifty steps to get to the water, I figured I should be able to get to the river and out of site in less than two minutes.

Sure, sure.

I planned the route I would take in my head and was about to make a run for it when I heard Eric.

"CAR!"

I didn't have my watch with me, so I counted out the seconds and observed the bridge. I needed to know how much time I had to climb up the bank again before a car got to the bridge and would be able to see me down by the washout.

"One thousand and one, one thousand and two, one thousand and three ..."

Rats!

I got to "one thousand and thirty-five" when a mini-van crossed the river. Thirty-five seconds didn't leave me much time to scramble back up the steep bank.

"CAR!"

I began my count, but this time only twenty-eight seconds passed until a telephone company truck appeared on the bridge.

"CLEAR," Eric screamed. And then again, "ALL CLEAR."

I leapt from the bank and scrambled down the washout, half sliding and half running. I slipped once on an exposed root and nearly lost my balance, but I managed to recover and narrowly avoided smashing the plaque against the rocks. When I got to the bottom, running became easy and I made excellent time. I was twenty feet from the water's edge when I froze.

The river bed, near the washout, was covered with damp silt. There was no way I could get close to the water line without leaving footprints everywhere. And that would be the most obvious sign of a hoax. I hadn't come this far to make such a stupid mistake.

"CAR! CAR! CAR!" Eric bellowed down at me from his perch upriver.

I spun around and bolted back up the bank. Counting off the seconds in my head, I scrambled like a maniac in the crumbling earth, and made it up and over the ledge just as a semi lumbered across the MacFie.

Whew. I collapsed in the grass, sweat dripping from every pore in my body. That was too close.

"CAR!" Eric screamed.

Thank goodness. I didn't even bother timing the vehicle as I lay panting in the sun. I considered my options. Only there weren't any. I had to approach the washout from the river.

"ALL CLEAR!" Eric cried.

What, already? I rolled over the lip and ambled down the bank again, careful not to drop the –

Oh, no! I had forgotten the plaque. How could I have forgotten *the plaque*? I spun around and groped my way back to the top. Snatching up the tablet, I listened for Eric's voice.

Nothing.

I turned and ran for the river. Without stopping, I went in the water up to my knees and plowed my way to the center of the washout, across from where Dr. Murray's hooks usually landed. With my heart slamming away at my chest, I repeatedly checked my position in relation to the dock behind me. It was vital that I place the plaque where it could be seen. Satisfied that I was in the right spot, I inched my way toward the waterline. As I leaned over to stick the stone tablet in the mud, the worst thing I could imagine happened.

"CAR!" It was Eric. "CAR, CAR, CAR!"

I thought I was going to puke. There was no way I'd make it back to the trees in time.

Then I had an idea.

I backed up until the river was at my waist, took a deep breath, and sunk out of sight in the MacFie. When I'd counted off thirty seconds, my lungs began screaming for oxygen. When I reached forty, I couldn't take it any longer. I poked my head out of the water and gasped for air. The bridge was free of traffic.

Smooth move, Cody.

I huffed and puffed my way back to the shore, leaned over, and slid a third of the plaque into the mud. I studied it for a few seconds. Nope, it looked too square – too much like a sign. I bent over, pushed it deeper, and yanked on it until it was at a rakish angle.

Satisfied, I sloshed my way back along the shore.

"CAR!"

I sighed. Not again.

Then, two seconds later I heard, "JUST KIDDING."

I couldn't see Eric, but I imagined him over in the trees laughing his face off. I shook my head and grinned.

"What happened to you?" Rachel surveyed my wet, bedraggled appearance with genuine concern.

"Oh, Rachel, you should have seen him," Eric said, back at our bikes. "It was so funny. Up the hill, down the hill. In the water, out of the water. I almost peed my pants."

Rachel had no way of knowing what had happened, so I explained how I had to get right in the water to avoid leaving footprints all over the shore. And how I had to hide underwater so that I wouldn't be seen in the river.

"Actually," Eric said, mounting his bike. "That was quick thinking. I never even considered the footprints. It would've given us away."

Rachel smiled at me as she climbed on her bike. "Piece of cake, right?"

"Just like I said."

CHAPTER 9

"Are you guys sure he's going to show up today?" Rachel asked. She was lying on her stomach and looking down at the dock from our hideout. "Maybe he's sick?"

It was half past nine on Wednesday morning and we were all anxious for Dr. Murray to find the plaque. He usually showed up around ten, but we were too excited to stay away. Plus, we all wanted to make sure the tablet had survived the night and hadn't been swept away by a flash flood or dragged away by a bear or something.

"Whew," Rachel said. "It's still there."

It was difficult to see it clearly from where we were hiding, but our tablet was where it was supposed to be – wedged in the mud, across from the dock.

"He might be sick of fish," I said, peeling the seeds away from a pine cone. "But he's not sick. He's a doctor."

"Doctors get sick." Eric was working on a breakfast of sunflower seeds. That was probably the least amount of food I had ever seen him eat.

"Heck, we don't even know if he's a doctor, doctor. He could be a P-H-D doctor."

"All doctors are P-H-D doctors," I said, flicking pine cone flakes into the air. "Otherwise, they couldn't call themselves doctors."

"No." Eric started getting frustrated. "What I mean is, Dr. Murray might not even be a people doctor. He could have a PhD in stars, and planets, and outer space stuff. He might be a whatchamacallit – a cosmetologist."

Rachel chuckled. "You think he's a make-up doctor?"

"What?" Eric scowled at his sister.

"You mean a meteorologist?" I said to Eric, helpfully.

"No," Rachel said, still squinting at either the dock, or the plaque. "That's a doctor of weather."

"Entomologist?" I said.

"Bugs." Rachel said.

"Astrologist?" I said.

"Nope." Rachel laughed. "But you're getting warmer."

"I got it," I said. "Dr. Murray's an astronomer. Right, Eric?"

Eric groaned. "You're both idiots."

Rachel and I laughed.

"Shhh," Eric hissed, "I think he's coming."

Eric and I flopped onto the ground on either

side of Rachel, making sure we were out of sight. We lay silent and listened. I heard nothing but the chirp of birds, the drone of insects, and –

"Yup," I said, "that sounds like his beater."

We couldn't see the truck from where we were hidden, but I could imagine him parking it, getting his gear out, closing the door, and walking to the dock.

"There he is!" Rachel cupped her hands together – I could tell she really wanted to clap them – and squirmed in place.

He appeared around the corner dressed in standard-issue grandpa clothes. It was like he was a model for *Old Man Quarterly*. His light blue shorts came down to his knees, where a band of white skin separated the shorts from his yanked-up socks. The socks were more or less the same color as the shorts. His loose, untucked shirt looked like wallpaper from some house in England. And to finish off the whole look, he had a cap on his head, which I can only describe as an old man hat. It looked like a cloth baseball cap with eighty percent of the beak chopped off.

Anyway, watching Dr. Murray turtle his way down to the dock was absolutely painful. I had no idea he moved so slowly. It was almost as if he knew we were there and was deliberately torturing us.

"Jeepers," Eric said. "It would be faster if he just rolled himself down to the dock."

"Hush," Rachel warned needlessly. There was no way he could hear us from where we were hiding.

After what seemed like a week, he finally made it to the end of the dock and began assembling his gear. My heart sped up as he attached the lure and got ready to cast.

"Man, I wish we had binoculars," Eric said, trying to focus on the end of the dock.

"You *do* have binoculars," Rachel pointed out, "and *you* should have brought them."

Down by the river, Dr. Murray swung the rod behind his shoulder and flicked the lure across the river. I heard Rachel hold her breath as the hook splashed in the water – six feet from the plaque.

"Gosh, that was close," Eric said.

Dr. Murray reeled in his hook – nice and steady, of course – and ignored the tablet. No bites for him and no bites for us. He did the same thing three more times, and with every cast across the MacFie, I prayed the old guy would see the light. I mean the artifact.

"Did you see that?" Rachel said. "The hook practically splashed the slate. How could he not see it?"

"Wait!" My eyes focused so hard they began

to burn.

He definitely paused after the lure hit the water *that* time. He had frozen for a moment before cranking the reel. But then the unthinkable happened – he caught a fish. Forgetting about the thing that had distracted him, he reeled in his lunch, or whatever meal he would have the dead fish for.

"I'm sure he saw it." Rachel squirmed in frustration. "Uuuugh."

We watched as he hauled the fish out of the river and let it flip flop on the dock. With his back to the bridge we could see him remove the hook, put the fish on a stringer, and place it in the pail of water.

"It's a jackfish," I announced, though probably no one cared.

"You can tell from here?" Rachel asked.

"Oh, sure," I said. "They have big heads and –"

"Quiet, he's casting again," Eric scolded, trying to avoid a fish-head lecture, I guess.

Dr. Murray realigned himself on the dock and flung the hook over the MacFie.

Plop!

This time it happened.

"He saw it!" Rachel grabbed Eric's arm and let go, all in less than a second. "I'm positive."

We watched as Dr. Murray froze and stared

across the river at the plaque. And when I say he froze, I mean *froze* – as if he was dead or something. The fishing rod stayed in his hand, and the line remained stretched out, like a long skinny finger pointing from the dock to the plaque. And Dr. Murray just stood there motionless, looking at it for an hour.

Okay, well, maybe not for an hour – but at least a minute.

Then he moved.

Dr. Murray reeled in the hook but kept his eyes locked on the plaque, almost like he thought it would disappear if he glanced away. Setting the fishing rod on the dock, he groped for his tackle box, and pulled something out.

"What's that?" Eric asked.

"Can't tell," I said. "It's small, whatever it is."

He had something in his palm, something black.

"It's a pair of binoculars," Rachel said.

He raised the binoculars to his eyes and began focusing on our plaque.

"See, Eric," Rachel said, "*he* brought *his* binoculars."

Eric ignored her.

The doctor lowered the binoculars and began surveying the area. Our heads duplicated each turn of his head. First he panned the whole east bank, from the bridge to the bend in the north. Then he turned around and examined the river bank where we were hiding. We shrank lower into the ground.

"What's he doing?" Rachel whispered, her breath tickling my face.

"I'm not sure." Our cheeks were pressed into the earth, and my nose was three inches from hers. "Maybe he's just paranoid, like all old people."

Eric must have chanced a peek, because he said, "He's looking at the tablet."

Rachel and I propped our heads up to watch. Dr. Murray was studying the slate through his binoculars again. Then he did a logical, beautiful thing – he spent four minutes sweeping the washout. Clearly, he was putting the pieces of the puzzle together.

"He's looking for more artifacts already," Eric said, pleased. "And he doesn't even have his mitts on the first one."

"I hope he doesn't find the little piece too soon," Rachel said.

"Ahh ... yeah about that." I cleared my throat. "I don't think he'll find that piece today. You see, it's still in my pocket."

"*What?*" Eric moaned.

I explained how with all the confusion yesterday, with the cars and so forth, I had forgotten about planting the little chunk we had broken off.

"It doesn't matter, Cody," Rachel said. "We can go back and bury that any time we want."

Satisfied that he wasn't being spied on, or set up by some hidden video show, Dr. Murray gathered his equipment and walked back to his conveyance. Every ten paces, he turned around and looked at the tablet, to make sure he could locate it when he crossed the river, I suppose.

"I wonder if he'll get to it again," Eric mumbled, "once he's crossed the river? That bush starts off pretty thick."

"Sure, he'll find it," I said. "Remember, he's an astronomer."

"That's right," Rachel added. "He can use the sun to find his way."

We remained on the grass and pine needles and waited for Dr. Murray's truck to cross the bridge. After six minutes, I was worried he wasn't interested anymore and had gone home. Or that he had Alzheimer's and forgot why he had left the river with only one dead fish.

"Maybe he's going to leave it to the pros," Eric said. "Maybe he's so convinced it's the real deal, he doesn't want to mess with the site – you know, tamper with the evidence."

"Could be," I said, hoping he was wrong. "But that would take a heck of a lot of willpower."

"Isn't the curiosity driving him crazy?" Rachel pushed a tangle of sweaty hair from her eyes.

I nodded, "Unless he's already crazy."

I had given up on the doctor and started to get up – I needed to stretch my legs – when Rachel yanked me back down.

"Wait!" She tugged on my hand. "That's him!"

I dropped to the ground and looked to the bridge. Sure enough, his truck was crossing the river. Only you couldn't say he was driving across the river: it was more like walking.

Eric groaned – loud, like a bear. "Doesn't he do anything fast? It's bad enough that he walks like he's pushing a piano, but does he have to drive slow too?"

"I bet he won't get to the plaque for at least forty-five minutes," Rachel said.

Eric's head bobbed. "I could actually go home, eat a bowl of cereal, and be back in time to see him yank it from the mud."

"Yeah, go," Rachel said. "And don't forget the binoculars."

"And bring me something to drink," I added.

"Me too," Rachel said. And before Eric could change his mind she added, "Hurry, before he sees you."

"And change your t-shirt," I said. "Even though we're hiding, he's going to see all that yellow when he gets up on the far bank."

Eric cursed us enthusiastically, hopped on his bike, and disappeared down the trail.

CHAPTER 10

There was not much to do but watch the empty washout after Eric left. I forgot Rachel was next to me and started daydreaming about the perfectness of this moment. I had a good feeling that things would work out for Cody Lint and his friends. The old doctor was about to stumble upon the hoax of the century, and everything was going according to ...

"Mom's last day is this Friday," Rachel said, pulling me back to reality.

What? I stopped searching the riverbank for Dr. Murray, and twisted my body so I could look at her. She was wringing her hands with worry.

Darn, I thought. We knew that our plan had to work fast, but this development gave everything a fresh urgency.

"Don't worry," I tried to sound confident. "This," – I pointed to the tablet down by the river – "is going to bring people to Sultana. I'm sure of it."

She squinted toward the plaque that would decide our future. "I hope you're right." Her voice grew so quiet I almost didn't hear what she said. "I really don't want to move."

"And I don't want you guys to leave either." I tried to lighten the moment and added, "I'm gonna get real fat if Eric isn't around to eat all the junk food Mom brings home."

Rachel laughed out loud. And not a phony laugh either – a good genuine laugh.

"The plan *will* work," I repeated, trying to sound as certain as I could, though I wasn't sure who I was trying to convince, me or her.

"Thanks, Cody. You're right. Our plan's great – it has to work." We returned our attention to the riverbank. I forgot about the daydreams. Now I was trying not to get nervous that Dr. Murray wasn't here yet. I figured she probably was too.

Ten minutes passed, and then Rachel spoke up again, sounding a lot cheerier than before. "Look. That was fast." She flattened her body against the earth, while I turned to look in the direction of her gaze. "Or, fast for Dr. Murray anyway."

There he was – Dr. Murray stood over the washout with his hands on his hips. He didn't seem to be in any hurry to get to the plaque, which was a shame. But it looked like he had left his binoculars in the truck.

"I hope he doesn't kill himself getting down to the river," I said. "Old people are kind of brittle."

"He's sure cautious." Rachel peered through the gaps in the brush and grass. "There he goes."

We watched him journey down the same crumbling bank of rock and earth and sand as I had. Only he was lucky, he didn't have to sprint. He stopped halfway and examined the collapsed bank. Then he continued. At first, I worried he saw my footprints, but the mixture of dry gravel and debris wouldn't reveal much. I hoped, anyway.

Then he did another funny thing.

"What the heck's he doing?" I wondered out loud.

His eyes swept the ground back and forth like a robot, all the way to the river, and then *into* the river. Rachel and I hadn't noticed before, but Dr. Murray had traded his shoes for rubber boots. And now he was trudging along the river toward the plaque. He kept his head down and continued to examine the wet earth as he approached the plaque.

"Man, is he good," Rachel said with admiration. "I think he's looking for footprints – your footprints. I bet if he saw even one print, he'd know the whole thing was a joke. And then ..."

"Look! He's going for it." I cut her off before she had a chance to get sad again.

Dr. Murray bent over and extracted the plaque from the sucking mud. I imagined the gooey sound of the slime falling away. He didn't stand up right away, but stooped over the river and rinsed the mud from the lower half of the plaque. Satisfied, he straightened and held the slate to his face.

"Look," Rachel marveled, "he's running his fingers over the glyphs."

Dr. Murray placed a bright yellow fishing lure next to the hole left by the slate. Then, he cautiously retraced his steps along the river's edge, around the wet mud, and up the bank. We watched him until he disappeared into the trees.

"So, now what?" Rachel asked.

"Now we wait."

"What if he just takes it home and puts it on the mantle?"

"He won't. You saw how careful he was. We left no signs at all that the stone is a hoax. And he's a doctor, and that's sort of like being a scientist. You know, curious and stuff. It would kill him not to know more about it."

"I suppose." Rachel didn't sound convinced. "Whatever he does with it, I just hope he does it quick."

We both stilled as we heard a rustle from the bushes behind us.

"Is it safe?" Eric whispered from inside a bush.

"Yeah," Rachel said. "The show's over."

Eric passed out cans of root beer, and we explained in detail how Dr. Murray had taken the tablet and how careful he was not to leave footprints near the site.

We calculated that if he took the plaque to some expert in the city, the earliest we might see any activity along the river was Friday or Monday.

We were wrong.

I had a hard time trying to get my usual twelve hours of sleep that night. So at eight o'clock, I got up, ate, and headed for the hideout. I knew nothing would be happening yet, but I didn't want to bug Eric or Rachel at such an ungodly hour.

As I emerged from the bush near our vantage point above the river, I nearly fell from my bike in surprise. Eric was *already* hiding in the shrubs.

"Get down! Quick!" he said. "Something's going on."

I shoved my bike deep into the woods, crawled over on my knees, and stretched out next to him. "How long you been here?" I said, panting. Eight in the morning was early for me, but for Eric it was unthinkable.

"Twenty minutes."

I looked around. "Where's Rachel?"

"She has to watch Gwyneth for a few hours. Listen. I was riding my bike over here, and two identical green mini-vans passed me on the highway."

"So? Lots of people have vans."

"I know," Eric said. "But they were following Dr. Murray's truck. I think he was leading them here."

"Have they crossed the bridge?"

"Yeah." Eric reached for the backpack and pulled out the binoculars. "We should see them by the washout any minute."

"Good thinking." I gestured to the powerful glasses with my chin.

Eric smiled and focused the binoculars on the opposite tree line. "I *do* think of everything."

We took turns scanning the far bank for the next ten minutes but saw nothing except birds. I was worried. Too much time had passed. It shouldn't take that long to walk to the washout. Eric reluctantly admitted that maybe it wasn't the doctor's truck he had seen.

When they finally did reach the clearing on the other side, we understood why it took them so long to get there.

Even without binoculars we could see the group fighting its way through the dense forest. And judging by all the boxes they were setting on the ground, they must have had an exhausting walk from the highway.

"Holy smokes!" Eric said. "There must be seven or eight people over there."

"And did you see at all the stuff they brought?" Every person, other than the doctor, was carrying either a bulky tool or a case of equipment. "These guys mean business."

"Some of the guys are girls." Eric passed me the binoculars.

I watched them converge at the top of the washout. Dr. Murray had his back to us and appeared to be explaining where he had seen the plaque and how he had retrieved it. A short blond-haired lady set up a video camera and began recording events. The camera followed Dr. Murray's finger as he indicated different areas of the site.

The expedition leader – or the guy we thought was the leader anyway – also appeared to be the oldest person in the group. Not quite as old as Dr. Murray, but probably around sixty. He had a gray mustache and gray hair, and was wearing a white shirt with khaki pants. The pants had a hundred pockets. It looked like he was asking lots of questions, which Dr. Murray answered either through words, or by pointing at the dock, the river, or the washout. Once he was satisfied with the debriefing, the leader gathered his crew together for what appeared to be a group meeting.

Dr. Murray stayed with the group, but retreated to the back of the pack. Each member of the team seemed to understand his or her role: when the leader clapped his hands, they dispersed like worker ants. The videographer never left the leader and she recorded the orders he occasionally shouted out.

"This is fantastic!" Eric said, watching two guys who were wrapping a yellow "DO NOT CROSS" tape around the washout. "They are *really* taking this seriously."

"Yeah," I said, weakly. "They sure are." And for the first time, I wondered if we could get in trouble for creating a hoax. What if the cops charged us for the time and money the guys across the river were wasting? What if Eric had to move away because his mom couldn't pay the fine? What if she got thrown in jail? Oh, man. What had we done?

I began to sweat.

"Can they do all this alone?" Eric asked.

"What do you mean?" I wiped my wet forehead.

"Well, can they just do whatever they want over there, without having to tell anyone?"

"You mean like the government or the newspapers?" I watched as the leader shuffled down the bank to the river bottom. "I suppose."

"Well," Eric said, "if *they* don't tell the papers

what's going on, who will?"

"Yeah, you're right. And it might take weeks for reporters to get wind of this project."

"Now you're thinking, Cody. But what can we do about it?"

"We can rat on them."

CHAPTER 11

"You stay here," I said, "And I'll go call the paper."

Eric looked worried. "What are you going to say?"

"I don't know yet. But I'll think of something by the time I get to a phone."

At least I hoped so.

I belly-crawled to my bike and left Eric at the observation post. As I pedaled down the trail, I wished I hadn't been so quick to volunteer to make the call. I mean, what was I supposed to say? I couldn't tell a reporter that a mysterious Egyptian plaque had been discovered because no one was supposed to know about it – other than Dr. Murray and his new friends. I also had to be convincing enough to get a reporter to hop in his car and race over to Sultana.

I considered going all the way back home so that I could call long distance and phone a big paper in the city. But I didn't know if they traced phone calls, so I abandoned that idea. Plus, I wanted to get someone's attention A.S.A.P. – like, right now.

The closest pay phone was the one bolted to the outside wall of the Rivercrest Motel & Restaurant, so that's where I headed. I decided on the way that I'd call the paper in Milner's Corner because that was still a local call. And since it was only a half hour away, I hoped I could lure the reporter into making the short trip.

I examined the few vehicles in the parking lot before I leaned my bike against the wall. One of the cars gave me an idea, and I knew instantly what I needed to tell the reporter. I looked up the number in what was left of the phone book hanging on a chain and made the call.

"*Star Times*," a female voice said after two rings.

"Could I please speak to a reporter?" I tried to deepen my voice, but probably sounded like a drunk.

The phone clicked, and another voice – a male voice this time – said, "Shaun Miles. How can I help you?"

"Yeah," I said, still using my phony voice, "what do you know about what's happening in Sultana?"

Mr. Miles paused. "What are you talking about?"

"Well, I think they found a body or something near the bridge. The bridge that crosses the

MacFie River."

"How do you know this?" Mr. Miles sounded suspicious. "Who found a body?" Maybe he had been sent on one too many wild goose chases in his career.

"I don't know *who* found it. But the cops are there right now with a bunch of other investigators. The whole area's taped up like a crime scene. So I assume it's a body. Or they could be shooting a movie too – lots of people are down there."

Mr. Miles sighed. "You don't sound very old, kid. Just tell me you're not pulling my leg. I'm pretty busy."

Oh, oh. He was on to me. "No, sir." I abandoned my deep-throat voice. "I swear. Just call the cops – they'll tell you. Or better yet, come take a look. You won't regret it. Something weird is happening in Sultana."

I hung up the phone without knowing one way or other if Mr. Miles believed me. He was cautious, which I expected, but I thought I was convincing. At least I hoped so.

I sat on the curb outside the diner, and waited for my next mark – that's what con artists call their victims. And I didn't have to wait long, either. Five minutes past nine, the door of the restaurant swung open, and two R.C.M.P. officers walked out and headed for their cruiser car.

Sultana didn't have a police station, so they must have been on patrol from Pine Falls or Pinawa.

I raced over to them on my bike and put on a good show of slamming my brakes. "Hey, are you guys going over to check out what's happening by the bridge?" I pretended to huff and puff, like I'd just raced down to the Rivercrest from the scene.

The two cops looked at each other over the roof of the car. "Why?" asked the female police officer. "What's happening by the bridge?"

My heart was pounding like mad already but I panted a few times anyway, before answering. "I don't know." I pointed down the highway to the MacFie River. "But there are tons of people there already. You can see them from the bridge. The whole area is taped up like a crime scene."

I heard the lady officer mumble something about "checking it out" to her partner and they got in the car. The other officer nodded at me through the window. "Thanks, kid."

The cruiser drove away toward the bridge. That made my day. I could imagine them crossing the bridge and seeing all the activity down by the washout. They might not stick around, but they'd have to go down and find out what the heck was happening. They couldn't deny *something* was happening in the normally quiet town of Sultana.

"Eric," I whispered from behind a pine tree. "Can I come over?"

He lowered the binoculars. "Yeah, but stay low. Real low."

I wormed my way next to him.

"They keep looking all over the place," he said, giving me an update. "And I don't know if the video lady has a zoom. We have to start being more careful over here."

He passed me the glasses. "So how'd it go?"

I told him about the phone call to the reporter and about my run-in with the law.

"That's brilliant, Cody. Now if the reporter is too lazy to drive over and simply calls the cops for information first, they'll say that there is no murder. And then if the reporter asks what's going on in Sultana, the cops will tell him the doctor found a three million year old artifact."

"Three thousand," I corrected.

"Whatever. This is perfect!"

As long as the cops don't throw us in jail, I thought.

Having left early, I was eager to see what the archaeologists were up to. And the first thing I noticed was that the investigation team was not eager to get too close to where we had planted the plaque. The entire perimeter – an area the size of a tennis court – was marked with the tape. And each person on the far bank was careful not to cross it.

"It doesn't look like they've done anything," I said, lowering the binoculars.

"It doesn't look like much, but they've been busy."

"Yeah?" I asked. "Doing what?"

"Well, see those guys up in the clearing?" He pointed across the river. "They haven't even left the upper bank yet. They've been sweeping the bush and the meadow with some kind of detector."

"Probably a metal detector," I said, squinting to see them.

Eric nodded. "That's what I figured. And see that big guy over there?" He needlessly pointed at the biggest guy in the washout. "Well, he's been scooping up water and testing it."

I was just about to ask what the leader had been up to when I saw the two cops approach the site. "Here we go," I said.

The cops stopped the first person they saw and were promptly directed to the boss. The boss was on top of the bank and it looked like he was showing two other guys how to mark a grid over the washout.

"The cops don't look happy," Eric said. "Look! She's yelling at the camera person."

The male officer pushed down the lens of the camera and the filming stopped. But it was the lady cop who was in charge and continued to do most of the questioning. I could totally imagine the conversation. A body? No. There's no body. Well what are you guys doing here? Someone found an object. What object? And so forth.

Suddenly, the leader shouted a command to one of the grid makers. The poor guy grabbed a big padded case from a stack of many padded cases and scrambled up the hill like his life depended on it. He delivered the case to the leader, who flipped a bunch of clasps, opened the lid, and proudly revealed our plaque.

"There it is!" I announced needlessly.

The female cop reached out her hand, but the case was yanked away and she was denied touching privileges.

Eric laughed. "Holy smokes. He's not even letting anyone touch it. It's like he thinks it'll crumble if someone picks it up."

"Well," I said, "it *is* three million years old."

The leader held up the case so that the cops could look at it better, but touching was not permitted. The officers looked at each other, asked a few more questions, and began taking notes.

Clearly, they thought a report was necessary.

The silence was shattered by the electronic squawk of the male cop's radio. We couldn't hear what was being transmitted, but whatever it was, it prompted the cop to twist his head and speak into the microphone attached to his shoulder.

"I wonder if that's Head Office asking if there's a crime scene?" I asked.

"PSSSSST!"

Eric and I spun around so fast we almost bashed our heads together.

It was Rachel. "Is it okay to come over there?"

"Yeah," Eric said. "But keep your bike out of sight."

She rolled her bike deeper into the bush, and then slithered toward us. She settled in beside Eric.

Her eyes got huge when she saw all the activity. "Jeepers, there's cops here!" Rachel laughed. "You mean this all happened in the last hour?"

"Yeah," Eric said. "Hey – look over on the bridge."

My head pivoted along with Rachel's. The bridge over the MacFie was lined with at least a dozen people. And every car that crossed slowed down to see what was going on.

"Word of this is going to be all over town in

about ten minutes," Eric said.

Rachel raised the binoculars to her face. "Make that five minutes. Mrs. Papenfuss is on the bridge."

Eric groaned, "Oh no."

"What do you mean 'oh no'?" I said. "It's a good thing. If Mrs. Papenfuss sees what's going on down here, she'll call everyone she knows. And she knows *everyone*."

"Yeah, but she doesn't know the facts," Eric whined. "She's just going to spread rumors."

"So what," Rachel said. "She can tell people whatever she wants, in fact, the weirder the rumors the better. If Mrs. Papenfuss wants to tell everyone that they're filming a movie, let her."

"Yeah. Good point." Eric grinned at the bridge. "Bring it on, Mrs. Papenfuss."

And another hour later, things got even better. The three of us were still monitoring events from our side of the river when Rachel noticed a flurry of activity up on the river bank, near the clearing.

"More people have showed up," Rachel announced. She adjusted the binoculars. "They must have followed the trail through the woods."

"Can you tell who it is?" Eric asked.

"Looks like some high school kids." She paused to study their faces. "Yeah, there's Bruce Webb, Stuart Webb, and even Lloyd what's-his-face."

"Who's the guy with the cowboy hat?" I

asked. I stuck my head above the brush so that I could see more. A lanky guy with a straw hat towered above the high school boys, but he was definitely not with them. He approached the washout and immediately separated himself from his escorts.

"Could be the reporter," Rachel said, passing the binoculars back to me.

I checked out the cowboy and watched as he talked to the cops and then the leader. "I think you're right," I said. And if it was him, he couldn't have come at a better time. The cops were still poking around and looking official, the investigators were still investigating, and even Dr. Murray looked pleased by all the attention.

"Yup. *That's* a reporter," Eric announced, as if he'd met a hundred other reporters.

The cowboy pulled a note pad from a satchel on his shoulders and began doing reporter-type stuff. First, he grilled the leader, and then the leader pointed to Dr. Murray, who was also questioned. When he was finished with the doctor, he hauled a camera from his bag and took photos of the washout, Dr. Murray, Dr. Murray holding the plaque, just the plaque, and finally the leader with Dr. Murray, holding the plaque and standing in front of the washout.

And then a bad thing happened. The reporter

pointed right at us.

"Oh, crap!" I said, shrinking down into the earth.

"What's wrong?" Rachel mimicked me and cowered lower.

"We have to leave," I said. "Right now! I think he's coming here."

CHAPTER 12

"How do you know that?" Eric asked.

"I just got a bad feeling that the reporter wants to take a picture of the washout from this side. After he took those photos from up on the bank, he started pointing over here. And I'm sure he's coming to get a few shots of the whole site. That's what I would do, anyway."

Eric frowned.

"It's not a big deal, Eric," Rachel added. "We just disappear for a while and let the guy do his thing."

"I suppose we could even go and lurk around the site," I said, "And act like we don't know anything. It only makes sense that every kid in town would be there."

Eric cheered up at the prospect of getting close to the action. "Yeah, I wouldn't mind seeing what all the fuss is about."

We laughed as we made our way back to the bikes.

We went across the river and hung out for a while with the other kids that came and went. We would have liked to have gotten right up close, but the cops began restricting access to the whole area, not just the washout. At first, the police gently guided the older kids away from the clearing, but when more people started showing up, it was obvious that the site would be trampled if something wasn't done.

So the cops chased everyone back to the highway. Well, everyone except Dr. Murray and the investigation team. Then a second police car arrived and the officers established a kind of command post near the highway. Anyone who dared to go into the bush or tried to sneak past the R.C.M.P. sentry was asked to stay away.

And we loved every minute of it.

The two cops from the restaurant began giving me looks that made me nervous, so I suggested we leave for a while. I know I was probably acting paranoid, but I didn't want the police to connect me with the hoax if things got messy. And believe me, things were getting messy.

On the way back to Sultana, we stopped on the middle of the bridge. When the bridge was free of cars, Rachel pulled the binoculars from her pack and examined the area near our lookout. "Cody, you were right," she said. "I can see the reporter standing in the woods."

"Is he taking pictures?" I asked, nervously looking up and down the highway for vehicles.

"He was. But now he's talking on a cell phone."

"I hope he's telling them to stop the presses," Eric said, "because he's got the story of the century to report."

"Car!" I warned.

Rachel slipped the binoculars back into her pack. "What do we do now?" She asked.

"Well, it wouldn't hurt if we ate," Eric said.

We rode past the Rivercrest on the way to my house – the parking lot was almost full! I would never have thought word could get out this quick, but clearly it had. Keep up the good work, Mrs. Papenfuss.

We returned to the lookout across from the washout two more times that day. Once at around four in the afternoon and again after supper. Word was all over town that an ancient mysterious artifact had been found by Dr. Murray, and it even had Mom and Dad chattering when they got home. Apparently, every person that stopped at the service station bugged Dad for details about the discovery.

I listened with a weird fascination as my parents gave me the facts. Obviously, *I* knew the facts, but I wanted to know what everyone else knew, if you know what I mean. The story Dad heard was that Dr. Murray had been fishing when he saw something poking out of the mud. Dad explained how the heavy spring rains must have shifted the earth around the artifact.

"Imagine," Dad said, leaning over his plate of spaghetti, "it could have taken years, maybe centuries, to find it if the river hadn't dropped."

"Or if Dr. Murray didn't like fish," Mom added with a grin.

"Or," I said, joining in on the fun, "if those Egyptians hadn't put it there."

"What?" Dad said.

"Huh?" I said.

"Egyptians?" Dad said, looking over at Mom. "Who said anything about Egyptians?"

Oh, oh. Me and my big mouth. "I ... uh ... heard some people talking and they said that there's some kind of writing on the artifact, and that it looks Egyptian."

Mom and Dad looked at each other. "Hmmm," he said. "I haven't heard that yet. That seems like pretty big news." I was relieved when Mom changed the topic – she was unhappy that the grocery store in Pinawa didn't have her favorite apples this week.

Anyway, nothing had really changed when

the three of us returned to the river that evening. The cops were still there and the area remained roped off, but for some reason, the researchers hadn't touched the washout. They never picked up a single rock or moved one shovel load of earth. What were they waiting for?

Well, it all came out the next morning in the paper.

I picked up the phone next to my bed after the fourth ring.

It was Rachel. "Did you see the paper?" She asked.

I looked at my watch – it wasn't even nine yet. "No," I said, "I just got up."

"Then don't move," she said. "I'll be there in fifteen minutes."

I groaned out loud, stumbled out of bed and did my best to eat, brush my teeth and get dressed. And all in less than ten minutes too. By the time I heard Rachel walking on the porch and ringing the bell, I think I looked pretty relaxed and alert.

"Why do you look all sweaty?" Rachel said when I opened the door. She brushed past me and into the room.

"Huh?" I mopped my face with my wrist. "Where's Eric?"

"He read the paper and crawled back into bed."

Lucky guy, I thought. I shook my head to demonstrate my disapproval.

Rachel opened her backpack and showed me the paper. I didn't have to flip through any of it because the story was right there on the front page.

Here's what it said:

Egyptian Artifact Discovered In Sultana

Did ancient Egyptians visit Canada? Well, that's what Professor Robert Bell and his team of investigators are going to find out.

On Wednesday morning, retired veterinarian Dr. Gerald Murray discovered a mysterious object on the bottom of the MacFie River. The object, which can best be described as a plaque or tablet, has markings on it that resemble Egyptian hieroglyphics.

Murray presented the plaque to the University of Manitoba's Ancient Studies Department for further analysis. Professor Bell, who is also the Department's resident archaeologist, said, "The text appears to be in Egyptian, but the tablet will undergo further analysis and dating before we can confirm its authenticity."

When questioned if the object could be a hoax, Bell answered, "There is no evidence at this time to suggest that the object is a fake."

Additional field excavations will take place on

Monday after the arrival of renowned Egyptologist Dr. Habib el-Medina.

"Wow," I said, examining the photographs next to the story. There was a picture of the plaque taken from six inches away, and a second picture of the washout shot from our side of the river. "I can't believe the university is getting another guy to come here."

"He's not from the university," Rachel said.

"Huh?" I was confused.

"He's from Egypt." Rachel tapped the name at the bottom of the page.

"Huh?" I was still confused. "Egypt?" I repeated the word slowly, like I'd never heard of the place.

"Yeah," Rachel said, "Dr. Habib el-Medina works for The Cairo Museum."

I still didn't understand what she was getting at. "How do you know that?"

"Because," Rachel said, "he's the guy who wrote that book I have."

"You gotta be kidding!" It was starting to sink in now. "You mean they're flying in a guy from Egypt?"

"Yes." Rachel nodded, pleased I was catching on. "He's coming to supervise the dig. And he's the one examining the plaque."

I barely heard what she was saying. The sound of blood pumping through my head was so loud, it drowned out her voice. We were all going to jail. Guaranteed. I mean, making a little stone tablet was one thing, but now that these guys were flying here ... man, were we going to be in trouble.

Yet, Rachel was all smiles. "Mom was told she had to work all weekend."

"Yeah? That's great," I said, and I meant it too. "How come?"

"Because our plan worked, Cody. All those people from the university are staying at the Rivercrest until the guy from Cairo – Dr. el-Medina – shows up. So Mom got more waitressing shifts at the restaurant to help feed them. She can't believe how lucky she is that she can work a few more days."

Yeah, she's lucky all right. Until we all go to jail.

With a sinking feeling in my stomach, I read the article again. "I'm kind of worried about all this testing stuff."

Rachel leaned in and examined the paragraph my finger indicated. "Why?"

"Well," I said, "if they do some carbon dating, or whatever it's called, they'll find out it was made three days ago, and not three thousand years ago."

"But maybe they can't do that in Manitoba." Rachel still sounded optimistic. "They may have to send it to Toronto, or California, or Egypt. It could even take months before they get results."

"I suppose," I said.

But it could also take hours, I thought.

That weekend was the most painfully slow weekend of my life. The three of us could not think or talk about anything except the plaque and the Egyptian who was on his way to Canada to look it over.

Eric couldn't have been happier. He thought we were going to change the history of North America with the tablet. Rachel just wanted to change her future so she wouldn't have to move. And I just wanted what Rachel and Eric wanted.

We returned to our lookout across from the washout as often as we could, but we tried not to look suspicious. Mom and Dad spent most of Saturday and Sunday puttering around the house doing yard work and didn't really expect me to stick around. But I made sure I had excuses ready, in case they asked where I was off to. Sunday evening was to be our last site inspection before the arrival of Dr. Habib el-Medina. It was nearing sundown when the three of us crawled across the pine needles and settled into our usual positions.

At first the whole area across the river looked the same as it had all weekend. The perimeter of the washout was still taped off, and one of the university investigators was reading in a lawn chair next to a tent. The team had set up a canvas shade and a screened tent in the clearing to stay out of the blazing sun during the day and to avoid the mosquitoes in the evening.

"Anything different?" I asked, waiting for Rachel to finish her survey and pass me the binoculars.

"I think so," she said slowly. "But –"

"But what?" I asked.

"Quit hogging the glasses," Eric said, extending his hand across my face.

Rachel ignored both Eric and my hands. "There's a guy over there just standing at the edge of the clearing."

"So? He's probably one of the researchers," I said.

"No. He doesn't look familiar," she said. "And it looks like he doesn't want to be seen."

Eric piped up again, "Come on, Rachel. Hurry up!"

I tried to see who Rachel was talking about in

the fading evening light but couldn't.

"Here, take a look." Rachel passed the binoculars to me.

Eric released a frustrated groan while I gloated.

I took the glasses, gave the focus dial a small tweak, and found the mystery man. He stood motionless in the shadow of a jack pine, a good fifty feet behind the lady who had been video-taping events earlier in the week. He definitely did not want to be seen. The camerawoman sat at the top edge of the river bank with her back to the forest and the stranger. I think she was doing a crossword puzzle.

"See him?" Rachel asked.

"Yeah, just barely. But how did he sneak past the cops?" I wondered out loud.

"He's not from Sultana."

"That's for sure," I said. His features were fuzzy, but he wasn't anyone I knew. He looked like a tall man, thin at the waist and broad-shouldered. His hair was black and he had a good suntan. "You know, maybe he's Egyptian too."

Eric couldn't take the suspense anymore. He snatched the glasses from my face and jammed the lenses against his eyes.

"Maybe that's Dr. el-Medina," Rachel said.

"He wouldn't have to lurk around, though,

like this guy. He would be taking charge of the whole place."

Rachel nodded.

"He doesn't look like a reporter either," Eric said, sounding happy to finally see something. "No camera. No bag. No notebook." He passed the binoculars to me again.

The suspicious man took two steps back and disappeared into the woods. For a split second his face had been visible in the setting sun. I had never met the man before, yet in that brief instant I thought there was something familiar about him.

"He's gone," I said, lowering the glasses. "Did he look like anyone we know?"

"Not to me," Eric said.

Rachel thought for a moment. "I don't think so."

I shook my head and tried to focus on a vague memory. "There's something about him that ..."

"– Maybe he gases up his car at your Dad's." Eric said. "Maybe you've seen him there."

"I suppose."

The three of us watched the lady doing the crossword puzzle for another fifteen minutes. It was a nice evening. The breeze from across the river kept the mosquitoes in the bush behind us, and the ground was still comfortably warm from another hot day.

I was about to suggest we leave, when Rachel grabbed my wrist. "Look!" She pointed around the bend in the river.

CHAPTER 13

"He's back." Rachel sounded worried.

The stranger – who, by the way, was starting to make me nervous – had worked his way back into the bush, and north toward the junction of the Red River and the MacFie River. He was out of site of anyone standing by the washout, but we could see him clearly.

I saw the outline of his body without the binoculars, but pulled them to my eyes anyway. "What the heck is he up to?" I murmured out loud.

"He's starting to creep me out," Rachel said.

Eric nodded. "Yeah, he's weird."

I agreed. There was something unnerving about the way he moved – or didn't move, I should say – as he studied the area. Using the binoculars I could see his dark eyes scanning the banks surrounding the river. I think if I was alone, I would have taken off a long time ago. But with Eric and Rachel there, I felt brave.

He reached into the chest pocket of his sand-colored jacket and pulled out a small pair of binoculars, similar to the type Dr. Murray had. He examined every inch of the river, the river bank and the tree line. We sensed when he got near our position and shrank deeper into the earth.

I stuck my head up when I thought he had swept past our spot, and focused on him with the binoculars. He was looking right at my face. "Shoot!" I dropped the glasses and wedged my face into the earth.

"What's wrong?" Rachel asked, her cheek still pushed against the fallen pine needles and grass.

"Did he see you?" Eric said, panic rising in his voice. "Did he?"

"Yeah." I tried to speak above the pounding rush of blood through my ears. "I think he may have."

Eric inhaled deeply through his teeth. "Rats!"

We let a minute pass before we chanced another peek. "Whew." Rachel brushed some dirt from her cheek. "I think he's gone."

I poked my head even higher. "Yeah, but where is he now?" It made me almost as jittery not knowing where the guy was. And the thought that I'd seen him somewhere before gnawed at the corner of my brain.

But where could I have seen him?

He wasn't with the research team. He wasn't a cop – well, he didn't look like one anyway. And I don't think he was a reporter. Other reporters and media people had showed up all weekend, and they weren't like this guy. Reporters walked around the site and asked lots of questions. But this guy looked like he was avoiding attention.

Rachel started to get up but Eric yanked her back down. "On the bridge! Hide!"

Man, was he fast. The intruder had worked his way back to the highway and was now standing on the middle of the bridge, over the MacFie.

Rachel looked around nervously. "Maybe we should get out of here?"

Eric and I nodded, but still hesitated to move. We were pinned down by the stranger. From his viewpoint on the bridge he'd be able to see us if we went for our bikes. We had no choice but to wait for him to get off the bridge before we could leave. And I hoped he did that soon – the mosquitoes were out now and starting to pester us, and soon they'd be unbearable.

"Why's he spending more time examining this side of the river than the washout?" I wondered aloud.

"Yeah." Eric confirmed my paranoia. "Why's he always looking over here?"

I chanced a peek toward the man. "Let's leave the second he's off the bridge. In case he decides to patrol this side of the river."

Eric and Rachel agreed, and we waited for our chance to escape. The bridge was three times as far

away from us as the washout, and I didn't think the
stranger's binoculars were as powerful as Eric's, so
I carefully watched him through the shrubs. After
five minutes of scrutinizing our side of the river, he
held open his jacket and began tucking the glasses
away. That was when I saw it.

"Oh my God!" I cried. "Quick, Eric, look at
his jacket." I fumbled to place the binoculars in his
hand. "What?" His fingers spun the focus, but it
was too late.

"What'd you see?" Rachel asked.

"A gun!" I couldn't believe what I was saying.
"The guy has a gun holster on his belt, under his
jacket. I'm sure of it."

Eric's eyes got huge. "Are you positive?"

Rachel breathed heavily. "Why would he
have a gun?" She tried to control her inhalations.
"Maybe he *is* a cop. But a whatchamacallit cop.
You know, undercover."

"I thought about that. But why would an
undercover cop sneak around the way he is?" I
pointed to the bridge with my nose. "He just
doesn't look like a police officer to me."

"Maybe he's a thief," Rachel offered.

"Yeah," Eric said. "Maybe he heard there
were ancient Egyptian relics here, and he thought
he could steal them."

It sounded far-fetched, but it was actually

the only theory that made sense. "We better be careful," I said, "until this thing blows over. Especially with that guy around ..."

Eric passed me the field glasses and I tried to find the stranger, but he had disappeared again.

"Let's get out of here," I said, already scrambling for my bike ahead of Rachel and Eric.

We pedaled like mad and made it to the safety of the highway. I turned around and saw him walk out of the boat launch access road.

"That was close," Eric said over his shoulder. "Another minute and he would've caught us coming out of the bush."

I took one last look. He had stopped moving and just stood there staring back at me. He was 500 feet away, so I wasn't scared, but it was still weird the way he seemed to want to get to us. I shuddered involuntarily and we continued down the highway to Sultana.

When it was time for us to split up, we agreed that I would come by their house in the morning. It wasn't safe anymore for anyone to be at the observation alone.

I didn't sleep much that night. Not because the intruder had scared me or anything, though that wasn't far off, but because he looked so familiar. Yet how could he be? I mean, if I had met anyone as creepy as him, wouldn't I remember them? He wasn't a teacher, he wasn't a coach, and he wasn't from Sultana. But he *did* have a gun, and he *did* look familiar!

But it was hard to keep thinking about him. There was a real excitement in the air Monday morning. It was like Sultana had woken from decades of boredom, and was now on the verge of something big. Mom and Dad chattered as they got ready for work. Dad had said that gas sales were up since the discovery, and maybe he sensed another good week. I wondered if the extra money would be enough to cover the fines they would get when it was revealed that their son was responsible for the hoax.

As I pedaled across town, I saw more people outside than I had all month. Neighbors were gossiping with each other, people were stopping their cars to talk to pedestrians, and so forth. Yup, there was electricity in the air.

By the time I was at the highway, I nearly fell off my bike. There must have been fifty cars parked in front of the Rivercrest. And not only cars, but big vans too, with TV station markings on the side and satellite dishes propped on the roofs. The largest vehicle was the size of a bus and proudly displayed CNN on all surfaces. I didn't watch the news much, but I did know that was an American station.

I began to feel sick again. This was getting out of hand. Seriously!

When I pulled up to Eric and Rachel's house, Rachel was already pacing the driveway while Eric sat, half-asleep, on the front steps.

Eric got up like a zombie and wandered over to greet me. "So, what's happening at the Rivercrest?" He rubbed his eyes with one hand and scratched his blond head with the other.

"It's nuts," I said, rolling to a stop. "Must be fifty cars there."

Rachel smiled. "Yeah, I thought there might be. Mom's making lots of extra money in tips, and she got called in two hours early today."

I told them about the TV station vehicles and all the activity on the other side of town.

Eric seemed to be fully awake now. "I can feel it too," he said. "It's like everyone knows something big is going to happen today, but nobody knows what."

I do, I thought. We're all going to prison.

We all pedaled to the hideout and dismounted our bikes 200 feet before the trail ended by the observation post. I didn't want to take any chances, so we hid the bicycles deep in the forest and approached the river from a different angle. Satisfied that the man from yesterday wasn't at the lookout, we settled in and began the stakeout.

It was only nine and the site was already buzzing with action.

After three days of waiting, the investigation team was ready to work. The washout had been marked off and sectioned into perfect one meter square parcels using strings and stakes. Screening stations had been set up well away from the washout to sift through the dirt and find more artifacts. One screen was at the bottom of the bank, and the other was up in the clearing.

"There must be thirty people over there," Eric said in awe.

Rachel had the binoculars again, so I had to squint to make out faces. In addition to all the familiar people from last week, two dozen new helpers swarmed the area. They looked like university students or volunteers. Some of them leaned on shovels, some worked the screens, while others kept records or shuttled items from the vehicles on the highway to the site.

"I don't see him," Rachel said.

I took the glasses and checked out the people on the other side. I wasn't relieved at all that Rachel couldn't see the stranger. I hoped she was wrong, and prayed that I'd see him shoveling dirt or making coffee. That would be more comforting than wondering if he was sneaking around the woods.

"Nope." I gave Eric a turn with his binoculars. "I can't see him either."

"That must be the professor from Egypt," Eric said after a few minutes.

Rachel and I watched as a short man emerged from the shade of the tent. He was with Professor Bell, the leader of the original team. Dr. Habib el-Medina – if that was who we were looking at – was a foot shorter than the Professor. He wore a tan-colored hat and a tan-colored suit that looked so new I wondered if he had bought those clothes especially for his trip to Canada.

The two of them ignored everyone and gestured to each other like excited toddlers. Moving to the top of the river bank, they continued their discussion, frequently pointing at the grid area below.

Eric giggled. "Here we go." He gave the focus dial a slight adjustment. "The reporters are starting to show up again."

Eric had the best view, but Rachel and I could see them too. Video camera crews and reporters suddenly appeared at the edge of the clearing and began filming, questioning, and reporting. Dr. el-Medina ignored the mayhem – like it was something he was used to – and continued to oversee the dig.

The reporters and media people were directed to an area near the tent. They were each provided a single piece of paper, and escorted by a lady to the different areas where they could film the activity. We could tell from the finger pointing and firm expressions the areas that were off limits. Any reporter who pointed questioningly at the grid was answered by a shake of the lady's head.

I held my breath as a CBC camera crew dared to venture to the grid, near where we had placed the tablet. Before they could cross even one square, two bulky guys pounced on them – we assumed they were the site security.

Eric laughed. "Man, they're taking this seriously."

"They better," Rachel said. "The history of North America is about to be changed."

We all chuckled in delight. But then our worst fear came true. The dirt crunched behind us and an unfamiliar voice cut through the morning air. "You have a magnificent view up here," it said.

CHAPTER 14

We spun over onto our backs. The creepy stranger was looming over us. Rachel gasped, but there was no point in trying to escape – he was too close. One of us could run for help, but all of us couldn't get away safely.

Plus he had a gun somewhere beneath his jacket. So even if he was super lazy and didn't feel like chasing us, he could still shoot us as we fled.

I decided to play it cool – like I always do.

"Yeah," I said. "It's a good spot to watch everything."

The stranger smiled and revealed two rows of perfect teeth. "Yes, it is." He had a thick accent that was probably Egyptian – but that was just a guess. "But I find it odd that you're hiding up here."

"We're not hiding," Rachel lied. "We're just more comfortable on the ground."

He smiled again – sort of an evil, yet charming smile. Kind of like when a handsome bad guy is about to shoot an unsuspecting good guy, if you know what I mean.

He turned and assessed Rachel before speaking to her. "It's comfortable on the wet and cold earth?" He ground his toe into the forest floor, for effect, I guess.

"What do you want?" Eric asked.

His dark gaze passed over me and found Eric. "I'm wondering why you've been hiding behind these shrubs and grasses for so many days?"

"We just got here, man." Eric sounded defiant.

"Really? The evidence tells a different tale."

"What are you talking about?" I said, wondering if I could tackle him while Eric and Rachel grabbed the gun.

"The ground by your heads is littered with enough sunflower seeds to fill a basket."

"So?" Eric challenged.

He looked at each of us for several seconds. "And your legs share a peculiar anomaly."

Eric looked at his legs. "Huh?"

"The skin on the back of your legs is darker than on the front. As if you've spent many hours lying on your stomach under the sun – perhaps right here?"

"Seriously," I said. "What do you want?"

The intruder ignored me and continued. "The trail through the forest has bicycle tire tracks from many visits to this point."

"So," Rachel said, "we like to come here."

He laughed. "Yes, you do indeed. Which

brings me back to the beginning. You enjoy coming here, but once you are here, you hide."

There wasn't anything we could say, so we didn't.

He took his time and studied us like he had some kind of magic X-ray device. "The discovery across the river is public knowledge and has been broadcast around the globe. It's no longer a secret. But you three are hiding from the archaeological investigation. Why is that?"

My brain worked through a dozen possible responses, none of which were logical, rational, or even probable. So I kept my mouth shut.

The intruder bent his knees and lowered himself to the ground. He was balancing on the tips of his shoes only a foot away from us. I had the urge to tip him over, roll him down into the river, and let him float back to wherever he came from.

He dropped his voice to just above a whisper. "As you've isolated yourselves from the world on the other side of the river, I wish to share something of interest with you."

I watched in horror as his hand slipped inside his jacket.

Oh, my God! I thought. This is it. He's going for his gun. He's going to shoot ...

"Please take this." He pulled out a single piece of paper from his inside pocket.

"What is it?" I mumbled, too scared to move my hand.

"It is the press release from the archaeologists." He waved the paper in his hand impatiently. "There will be a public meeting later today inside your town's community hall, and I think perhaps you three should attend."

"What do you care?" Eric said.

"*I* don't care." The stranger stretched back to his full height. "But clearly you find this dig fascinating, and I thought you might also want to know the *truth* about what has been unearthed."

There was something about the way he said "truth" that made me cringe. When I took the paper from him, he turned and walked down the trail. None of us said anything as we tried to absorb what had just happened.

Eric broke the silence first. "What's his problem anyway?"

"Never mind that," I said. "What the heck does he want? Who is he? And why does he look so familiar?"

"And why does he have to be so creepy?" Rachel threw a stone down the trail, where he had vanished moments before.

I rolled over onto my stomach again, unfolded the paper, and read it.

"What's it say?" Eric asked. He was still on

his back.

"Exactly what Creepy told us. There's going to be a public meeting at the hall after lunch to explain what's been found and what's going to happen." I passed Eric the sheet.

"Are we going to go?" Rachel asked.

"We might as well," I said. "We should be safe there with all the people around."

"But what if it's a set-up and this notice is a fake?" Eric rolled up the paper and poked a small pile of sunflower seeds. "He might be luring us into a trap, so he can kill us."

"If he wanted to kill us," Rachel said, "he could have done that right here, or in the bush. It wouldn't make sense to make us go into the middle of Sultana, where there might be witnesses."

"And we'll know if something's fishy as soon as we get there," I added. "If we don't see TV station vehicles, or reporters all over the street, we can leave."

We stayed at our lookout and monitored the activity across the river. We didn't say very much as we watched the dig. None of us really felt like being there anymore, but we had nowhere else to go until the press conference, so we stayed.

"I feel kind of dumb," Rachel said, "still hiding."

"I know what you mean," I said. We had made it such a habit to hide from people on the other side, it never occurred to us that once the plaque was found and made public, we didn't have to conceal ourselves.

Eric agreed. "Yeah, Creepy had that right, anyway. We could run up and down this side like monkeys, and it wouldn't matter to anyone."

"Hiding like this," I said, indicating the shrubs which were shielding us, "*makes* us look suspicious if we're seen."

"Let's get out of here." Rachel got up and brushed away the debris from her legs.

After a lunch of microwaved hotdogs and milk, we walked over to the community hall for the press conference. Since the hall – officially named The Sultana Multiplex – was on Park Avenue and only a block from my back door, we didn't take our bikes.

As we cut across Mr. Durupt's lawn and through Mrs. Malbazza's yard to the parking lot, we could see something big was happening at The Multiplex.

The residents of Sultana all lived within walking distance, so there weren't many local cars in sight. But the two-acre field in front of us had nearly hit full capacity. TV station vehicles packed the gravel lot that surrounded the low, steel-wrapped building. You would have thought they were covering the Olympics.

"Jeepers!" Eric stopped under a huge oak tree at the edge of the parking lot. "Look at all those satellite dishes."

"I don't see our friend anywhere," I said, trying desperately to spot him among the throng of reporters, camera crews, and technical people.

Eric shrugged – probably already forgetting our new enemy.

As I stood there, trying to take in the action, I was suddenly overwhelmed by all the people who had wasted their time to come to Sultana. And I couldn't take it any longer. "Man, are we in trouble." I shook my head.

Eric looked at me like I'd just grown horns.

"No, we're not," Rachel said. "We're the only people who know we made the plaque, and we're not going to tell anyone. And there's no way *they* can figure it out." She waved an arm across the lot in case I had forgotten who "they" were.

I guess I didn't look convinced, so Eric jumped in. "And even if they do find out it was us – which they never will – they can't do anything to us because we're kids."

I had heard that before from other people, but I found it hard to believe that we could create such chaos and not suffer any consequences. And for a split second I wondered if we would get sent to some weird youth prison like "juvie".

Rachel turned and looked me in the eyes. "And if they really do find out it was us –"

"Which they won't," Eric interrupted.

"– they can't make a big deal out of it, because they'll just look stupid for letting a bunch of kids fool them."

"She's right, Cody," Eric said, still trying to help. "Just be cool."

"I suppose." I wondered if Eric and I could go to the same juvie jail. It wouldn't be so bad if Eric was in the same cell with me. At least then we could play checkers together and shoot baskets in the exercise yard. If he moved away next week, I'd probably never see him again.

I realized I was daydreaming, and that Rachel and Eric were looking at me like they wanted an answer. I snapped out of it and recovered my cool. "Huh?"

Eric sighed and, I think, repeated himself. "Should we go in right now? Or hang back and see who shows up?"

"Yeah, let's wait around for a while," I said, not wanting the creepy man from Egypt to sneak up on us again. "I don't think we need front row seats."

Eric nodded and headed toward the largest cluster of camera people.

Despite what Rachel and Eric had said, I didn't feel that much better. Maybe this mess could end without Eric and his sister needing to move away, and without me doing hard time at some dirty detention centre. But I sure doubted it.

CHAPTER 15

The press conference was nuts.

They had to try to fit everyone in the building, which wasn't easy because no one thought so many people would show up. Every person in Sultana who wasn't at work that day was sitting in a folding chair in the community hall – there were even people sitting on the floor. And every reporter and camera crew battled for the best position to view the event.

We stood in the back corner, near the coatroom, and watched various TV crews make demands of Mr. Baker, the unofficial caretaker of the building. The lights weren't bright enough for CNN. CBC wanted extra chairs at the front. And two shifty-looking guys, who sounded German, demanded more extension cords. It took a while for Mr. Baker – who's kind of deaf anyway – to figure out what they wanted. In the end he pointed to the electrical room and told them to help themselves.

And every five minutes another stack of chairs had to be set up for the out-of-towners.

Word had spread far beyond Sultana and people were pouring in from all over the area. Like I said, it was nuts!

At the far end of the hall, four long tables had been placed next to each other to make one elongated head table for the speakers. We recognized most of the people. Dr. Habib el-Medina waited patiently at the centre, next to a sweaty, nervous-looking Professor Bell. Occasionally, I saw the professor lean over and whisper something to Dr. el-Medina, who responded with either a nod or shake of his head.

The other members of the team flanked the doctor and professor on each side. The university was represented by the big, water-sampler guy and some of the other site investigators, while The Cairo Museum was represented by two Egyptians who we couldn't identify.

We bumped our way through the gauntlet of wires and people without tripping, and found three chairs next to an emergency exit. The door had been propped open with a plastic milk crate in a failed attempt to ventilate the stifling bingo hall air.

Rachel cupped one hand over her mouth and said, "I think that's the plaque." She nodded toward the front of the room.

I craned to see around a photographer who

was wearing a hundred cameras around his neck. Well, maybe not a hundred, but you know what I mean. Anyway, he was jostling for the best floor space with our local cowboy reporter, who didn't feel like budging.

"Yup, that's it," I said. The plaque was on the table in front of Dr. el-Medina in the same padded case we'd seen before. And it was proudly propped open so that pictures could be taken before, during, and after the meeting.

I should have been relieved that I couldn't see Creepy, but I had a feeling he was somewhere in the building.

Finally, Professor Bell flicked on the microphone in front of him and pulled it close.

My heart began to pound.

"Ladies and gentlemen," the professor began. His voice traveled through the hall loudly and clearly. "If everyone could please get settled, we'll begin."

The room grew quiet, and after a minute the only sound we heard was the electronic hum of video and tape recorders.

"We are here to provide the residents of Sultana, and the media, with information related to an artifact that was discovered along the MacFie River last Wednesday morning."

Professor Bell paused and wiped his forehead with a white handkerchief. A few reporters thought that was worth a picture and some camera flashes went off.

He continued, "First, I will introduce these people who you see next to me. Then we will each make a statement on the item before us. And finally, when we're done, we will try and answer any questions from the media and address any concerns from the public."

Professor Bell spent ten minutes identifying each person at the front of the room. According to him, everyone was either a doctor of something, a professor of something, or a member of some scientific organization. After rattling off the accomplishments of the last person at the table, he pushed the microphone toward Dr. Habib el-Medina.

"Thank you, Professor Bell," Dr. el-Medina said. I noticed he had a slight British accent. "As you are all aware, a tablet was found on the outskirts of this village last week."

He paused and picked up a pair of white cloth gloves from the table. He carefully put them on his hands, and then extracted our plaque from the case. Tilting it slightly, he held it for the room to see. This must have been some kind of a signal for the photographers because flashes burst around the hall.

Eric poked me in the ribs and grinned. It was almost like *we* were standing up there and the flashes were applause for us. It was all very cool, if you know what I mean.

"The tablet, as you can see, has been inscribed with Egyptian pictographic symbols – more commonly referred to as hieroglyphics, or hieroglyphs." He delicately ran a white finger across the surface.

"These symbols have been translated by my team from The Cairo Museum." He paused to take a swallow of water from the bottle in front of him. "And the translations have been validated and confirmed by other leaders in the field of Egyptology." He scanned the room like he was daring anyone to challenge what he was going to say.

"The tablet indicates that ancient Egyptians traveled up the Mississippi to the center of Canada."

Dr. el-Medina had barely said the last word when the room exploded. The three of us jolted in surprise as even more flashes went off – and for much longer this time. Reporters shouted questions, unsuccessfully trying to outspeak each other, while gasps rose around them.

"Outrageous," someone cried.

"I knew it!" screamed Mrs. Malbazza.

"Please," Dr. el-Medina said. "Please, everyone. Quiet."

The rumble in the community hall gradually and reluctantly fell away.

"The glyphs, although rudimentary and simple, are quite clear in their meaning. Our consensus is that the message was composed and crafted by a lesser scribe – perhaps an apprentice – or by an officer or official who had observed the work of a scribe."

A reporter in the crowd stood up and burst out, "How'd they get here?"

Dr. el-Medina acknowledged the man with a nod. "Yes, I am getting to that. The tablet also describes a journey north on the Mississippi River – probably originating in the Gulf of Mexico – and then down the Red River into this area. Once in Canada, however, they found themselves unable to survive in the harsh Manitoba winter."

Again, silence engulfed the crowded room. Probably everyone was imagining the November winds pounding the unprepared Egyptian explorers.

"The message on this tablet is not an impersonal account of taxes, or a record of the spring inundation in the Nile valley." Dr. el-Medina's voice softened. "This is a personal message from a doomed group of Egyptian explorers. It is a story of an ocean crossing, adventure, and discovery in a strange land. And tragically, in the end, a tale of despair and sorrow as they realize they will never return home."

"This is their final prayer for peace in the afterlife." Dr. el-Medina held the plaque in front of him and touched the last four glyphs. "Osiris, have mercy on our souls."

Eric elbowed me again to get my attention. With a twist of his head he pointed to Mrs. Webb, who was sitting ten feet away from us. I followed his gaze and saw tears were running down her cheek. I tried not to look at Eric again because I wasn't sure I could hold back my laughter.

Dr. el-Medina passed the microphone to Professor Bell. "Thank you, Dr. el-Medina. Now, does anyone have any questions?"

A man who must have been sitting on the floor jumped up and said, "How do you know that the tablet isn't a fake?"

The Professor cleared his throat. "There is absolutely no evidence to suggest the plaque is anything but authentic."

"Yeah," the same guy said, "but how do you know this isn't an elaborate hoax?"

"For a prank to be appreciated by a prankster, it has to be discovered. Right?"

Heads nodded.

"Therefore, I suggest it's unlikely that someone would create a tablet of this quality, and then simply cast it into the river with the hope that it will one day be discovered during a dry year. Even a patient prankster wants some satisfaction."

Polite giggles rippled through the hot air.

"Has the tablet been tested in any way?" asked a reporter who I couldn't see.

"Oh, yes. Unfortunately, the tablet could not be accurately carbon dated because there is no organic material present. The clay in this area is so pure, these explorers had no reason to add straw or ashes to improve on quality – as they normally would in Egypt. And without any traces of living, organic material, we were unable to conduct a proper carbon-14 analysis."

A grumble of doubt rose from the crowd.

"But," he quickly added, "the clay covering *has* been tested and identified, and although common, it is from a strata that is no longer found at grade."

A farmer stood up and yelled, "What the heck does that mean?"

Everyone laughed.

"It means," the Professor said slowly, "that the clay used for this tablet is old, came from deep in the ground, and has not been exposed to the atmosphere for thousands of years. In other words, it is not the same clay that you grow your carrots in."

More laughs.

"Furthermore," he continued, "geologists have examined the slate backing, which makes up the spine of the tablet, and have stated that it could only come from a deposit in southern Louisiana."

He waited for the significance of this to sink in. But it didn't.

So he helped everyone out. "A deposit that happens to be adjacent to the Mississippi River."

Murmurs of understanding echoed through the hall.

An older reporter wearing a suit stood and pointed a pencil in the air. Professor Bell gave him permission to speak with a nod.

"So you people are saying that Egyptians landed on North America *before* the Europeans? How is that possible?"

"First of all," the Professor said, "Vikings had come to America long before Europeans did. Secondly, is it really such a stretch to imagine that Egyptians crossed the ocean? Ladies and gentlemen, the Egyptians had very capable ships and they were *not* frightened of water. In fact, they controlled the annual floods of the Nile with inconceivable precision and engineering for over three thousand years."

The Professor paused and took another swallow of water.

"And let us not forget," he went on, "that they constructed pyramids that have lasted millennia. So why on earth couldn't they build a ship robust enough to cross the Atlantic? The Europeans did it, the Vikings did it before them, and now we have evidence that Egyptians did it before that."

The audience absorbed and processed these facts in silence. Eventually, heads began to nod. I mean, it was – like the Professor said – possible, probable, and even logical that Egyptians traveled through Manitoba over three thousand years ago.

Eric leaned in so only I would be able to hear him. "They're falling for it!" he whispered.

Another person who I couldn't see – a lady this time – asked, "So what will you do now?"

"Dr. el-Medina and I believe that this tablet is only one of many. We feel the entire journey up from the southern United States may have been documented on slate tablets similar to this. Therefore, we will be continuing with the dig until we find those records."

Some of the local residents nodded – they were probably excited by the idea of more action in the area.

"We are especially eager to find material organic in nature – perhaps bones, or wood – so that the age of the site can be confirmed."

"What if you don't find anything?" a CBC reporter asked.

"We have spent the past week studying the area where the MacFie and the Red River converge." Professor Bell looked over at Dr. Habib el-Medina for support. "And we believe that this site came to be the last camp of the Egyptian exploration team. If we are correct, there has to be more evidence. And we are determined to find it."

I looked at Eric and both of us cringed – there was nothing more to find. It was then, as I gazed past Rachel and into the crowded hall, that I found myself looking right at Creepy.

And he was looking right back at me.

CHAPTER 16

It was weird.

For whatever reason, I decided to look across the packed room. The sea of heads that had been rocking gently back and forth like waves parted, leaving a visible gap through which I could see the other side. And it was at that exact instant that I saw Creepy. He was standing in the shadow of a steel beam, under a faded photograph of the Queen, looking like he didn't want to be seen.

And here's the part that made me shudder. He wasn't looking at the Doctor, or the Professor, or any of the other panel members – which is what all the normal people were doing – he was staring at us. At me!

Our eyes locked, and I knew in that instant I *had* seen him before. I mean, he didn't feel familiar in the sense that I'd played floor hockey with him, or sat next to him in Church, or washed his car for him. But I'd *seen* him before. Where, though?

"What's wrong, Cody?" Rachel asked.

"Yeah," Eric said. "You look sick."

"He's here," I answered abruptly. "Under the

Queen." I was still trying to latch onto that vague memory.

Eric's head snapped to the left, but it was too late. People had started to get up to leave and shuffling bodies now blocked our view of the other side.

"I don't see him ... he's probably gone now," Eric said. He didn't seem as worried as I was that someone was stalking us. "I wish I had a camera. It would be cool to get a picture of that doctor dude holding our plaque."

I nodded even though I barely registered what he was saying – my brain was still fishing for a clue, anything that would jostle my memory. Think ... it was something Eric had said ... think ...

"That's it!" I shouted over the noise of chairs banging into each other. Grabbing Eric's arm, I pushed him toward the emergency exit. "We have to go to your house. Right now!"

Rachel looked confused. "What's going on?"

"I'll tell you outside," I yelled. "Come on!"

I ran through the gauntlet of vehicles until the three of us were near the tree line at the edge of the parking lot. As we tried to catch our breath, I explained my revelation, and why we needed to go back to Eric and Rachel's house. Rachel's eyes grew bigger and bigger as she listened.

"Well, let's go check it out," she said.

Twenty minutes later the three of us were sitting on Rachel's bed.

"Oh my God," Rachel said. "Cody's right!"

She had her Egypt book open on her lap and we were looking at the photograph of the hoax site in Australia. Her finger was on the same black-and-white picture of the pranksters we had first looked at a week ago. The hoaxers stood next to their cliff art, surrounded by experts, reporters, and other unidentified people. And there, among the unidentified, we saw Creepy.

Eric pulled the book from her lap and held it up to his face. "Yeah, there's no doubt about it. That's our guy. He's way younger here, but it's him all right."

I took the book from Eric and studied the photo, but it provided little useful intelligence. He stood alone at the back left corner of the photo – almost like he didn't want to be included. But he couldn't escape the wide-angle lens of the photographer. His expression was neutral and gave nothing away.

I tapped his face with my finger. "Why is this guy always lurking around these sites?" I said. "He's not a cop because cops only care about stuff in their own countries. Right? And Creepy has showed up in two countries already."

"What about Interpol?" Eric asked, returning to the big barber chair. "He could be a special agent for the International Police."

Rachel took the book back and re-examined our friend. "I don't think Interpol cares about archaeological discoveries. Especially if they haven't even been confirmed as authentic."

"Well," Eric said, "then maybe he's just an Egyptian who's fascinated with hieroglyphics and archaeology. Maybe he's a collector."

"Eric, the man has a gun!" Rachel said.

Eric swung his legs over the side of the chair. "So? Indiana Jones had a gun."

"I thought he had a whip," I said, still looking at the photograph.

"Indiana Jones had a gun *and* a whip," Eric said. "Remember when that huge guy was going to slice him up with a sword? And the guy was showing off because he thought Indiana Jones only had a whip. So Indiana Jones pulls out a gun and shoots him – BANG! Remember?"

Rachel and I looked at each other.

"Whatever," she said.

"I still like the thief theory," I said. "Somehow he gets word of these discoveries and quickly flies to the country where the items are found. And he has to get to the dig sites fast – before they become a big deal – so that he can steal the artifacts while security is still light."

"I suppose," Rachel said, "that would explain the gun and his sneaky behavior. But –"

"But it doesn't explain his fascination with us," I said. "Right?"

Rachel nodded.

Eric threw both his legs over the backrest, so that he was upside down. "Maybe he's watching us," Eric said, "because *we're* the ones who've been acting sneaky. And maybe he thinks that we know something about the plaque that nobody else knows."

"We do know something no one else knows," Rachel said. "We made it. And after today it'll probably be locked up tight in a museum in Winnipeg."

"Which means that Creepy will have nothing to steal," Eric said, upside down and looking creepy himself. "So he can go back to Egypt empty-handed."

"That's so sad." Rachel started to smirk.

"Huh?" I said. "What is?"

"That he came all the way here and can't steal a souvenir to bring back for his bosses."

This time Eric responded with a "Huh?"

Rachel leaned forward. "Why don't we make one more tablet and this time we'll set it up so he can steal it." She chuckled mischievously. "We've got plenty of slate shingles, and we know where to find the clay."

I laughed, imagining the trouble he would be in when he presented his evil boss with a roofing tile from New Orleans. "And this time let's make pictographs that say, 'the person who brought you this tablet is the world's biggest moron.'"

"I'm not sure we can find a glyph for 'moron'," Rachel said with a wry smile. "But let's do it."

Eric righted himself again. "And let's do it now," he said, getting excited. "Before Creepy leaves town."

Rachel and I pedaled through the dust clouds on the gravel road leading out of town. Eric wasn't with us. Mrs. Summers had called the house and asked Eric to come by the Rivercrest and drop off her camera. She wanted to take pictures of some of the TV reporters who kept dropping in to question the coffee shop patrons. He wasn't happy about it, but it also meant things were booming at the restaurant. Anyway, he'd join us when he was done.

With all the vehicles pouring out of Sultana,

Rachel and I couldn't talk much on the ride. Normally, we would be waving to the people we knew, but this time we had to really concentrate on avoiding the ditch and the cars speeding past us.

I was relieved when we finally left the gravel and began our ride down the access road to the new barn. I hoped no one in the cars recognized us, or they might start wondering why Rachel Summers and Cody Lint were sneaking around an unfinished dairy barn.

"Oh, good," Rachel said, leaning her bike against a pile of steel beams. "They haven't filled in the trench yet."

We could tell someone had worked on the site recently because more materials had been dropped off. But lucky for us they hadn't made any progress on the trench that split the barn down the middle. Except the ladder and shovel had disappeared and it took us ten minutes to locate them.

"Should we wait for Eric?" I started to set up the ladder again.

Rachel shrugged and dropped the shovel in the pit. "I don't think he'll care if he misses the dig."

I followed her down the trench to where we had found our first batch of clay. Rachel unfolded a plastic bag from her pack while I carved into the damp clay wall. We had lots of light this time because the sun was still high in the sky above us.

I was scooping the last handful of clay out of the wall when, suddenly, I couldn't see a thing in front of me. It was like someone had put a rock in front of the sun. We looked up and saw a silhouette blocking the entrance above us.

"What are you doing down there?"

I dropped the shovel – I recognized that voice and that shape. Creepy was towering over us. And we were trapped. The ladder was our only means of escape and all he had to do was pull it up and we'd be dead.

"What do you want?" Rachel shouted. She was trying to sound brave, but I heard the shudder in her voice.

"I don't want anything from you," he answered.

I wished I could see his face, but it was shrouded by shadows.

He continued: "I have everything I need to know now."

Rachel and I looked at each other, neither one of us sure what that meant.

"Don't be alarmed," he said. "I have something for you that you'll find interesting." Even with the sun over his shoulder, I saw his hand tap his jacket pocket, the same place I knew he kept a gun.

"We don't want anything from you!" I answered.

The stranger laughed. "Oh, I think you'll want

this. Now, please come out. I'll drive you back into town." He sounded calm, not menacing at all, but isn't that what they always say about psychos?

I was sure he was going to shoot us as soon as we climbed the ladder. I just couldn't figure out why.

"Look," Rachel screamed, "if you're going to kill us, just do it! Stop playing games!"

I tried to warn Rachel with a look – what if she really *did* provoke him into shooting us right then and there? – but it was too dark. But then something strange happened. Creepy was shaking his head at us, clearly about to say something, when he collapsed to the ground like a sack of hammers. We couldn't see where he fell, but at least it wasn't on us.

Then, another shadow blocked the sun.

CHAPTER 17

"Good timing, eh?" It was Eric, and now *he* was standing on the lip of the trench. He held something long in his hand – it looked like one of those steel pipes from the site.

Rachel and I scrambled up the ladder.

"Get his gun," I said to Eric. "And we better tie him up quick!"

Eric ignored us and bounced around the site, waving his weapon in the air and whooping like a mad man. "I really *am* like Indiana Jones, always arriving in the nick of time."

"Yeah, yeah. Whatever," Rachel said. "Just help us find something to tie him with."

We ran about the construction site frantically searching for something to bind Creepy's arms and legs. I was about to give up when I noticed a plastic clothes line behind one of the construction trailers. I worked it loose and sprinted back to Eric, who had finally settled down a bit.

The man moaned as the three of us dragged his huge body to a nearby utility trailer. He continued groaning as we propped up his back against the rear tire and tied him to it. It wouldn't hold him forever, but at least we would have time to get away if we needed to.

Rachel took the gun from Eric and held it away from her with two fingers, like she was carrying a dead rat. Her arm shook as she placed it in her pack.

"I think he was about to kill you guys," Eric said, clearly pleased with his action hero timing.

"I'm not so sure about that anymore," I said, hovering over the stranger. For some reason, he didn't look as dangerous now that we had him wrapped up and unconscious.

"Are you kidding me?" Eric said. "He must've followed you guys all the way from town." He pointed to a car with rental license plates sitting a hundred feet away. "And why would he do that, if he wasn't planning on shooting you?"

"But *why* would he want kill us?" I said. "It doesn't make sense. I mean, it would make sense if we had a whole stack of ancient tablets with us and he wanted to steal them. But we've got nothing."

Rachel kicked his shoe lightly and stepped back. "Let's ask him," she said. But he only groaned and his head flopped to the right.

"Huh?" Eric said.

"Well, why not?" She cautiously tapped his foot again. "He can't do anything to us now. So let's wake him up and find out what his problem is."

"That's a good idea," I said, poking his unconscious form with the pipe Eric had used to clobber him. "He keeps asking us dumb questions. It's time we got some answers from him."

Eric found an empty pail of tar, flipped it over and sat on it. Then he joined us and began poking the man with a stick.

Our prisoner's chin flopped forward and rested on his broad chest.

"How hard did you hit him?" Rachel asked.

"I don't know," Eric said. "Medium."

Rachel frowned. "What does that mean?"

"It means I hit him *medium* hard. Not *super* hard."

"What if he dies?" Rachel asked, continuing to tap him.

This time Eric groaned. "I didn't hit him *that* hard. His head wasn't even bleeding. Ask Cody."

I shook my head. "There was no blood."

Rachel looked relieved. "HEY, MISTER!" she yelled. "Please wake up. Pretty please!"

His eyes opened and then rolled way up like he was looking for something under his forehead. A second later they slammed shut again.

"Darn!" I stood up. "I'm going to go check out his car."

His car didn't provide any useful information

about his identity. Some road maps were on the front seat, but otherwise the vehicle was 'clean', as they say. On the rear seat I found two water bottles and took them back to our sleeping mystery man.

We shared the one bottle of water among the three of us and tried to revive him with the other. Rachel gently poured water into his half-open mouth, but he sputtered it back out. Eric tried another tactic: he ran around making as much noise as he could, but that didn't work either.

Eric stopped to catch his breath. "It's too bad we don't have anything super stinky to wake him up with."

"What are you talking about?" Rachel said.

"Well, on TV they always shove something stinky under a boxer's nose when he gets knocked out." Eric scratched his own nose. "That *always* makes them snap out of it."

"Sure it would," I agreed. "But we don't have anything like that, so forget about it."

"Well, you know something stinky..." Eric started.

I recognized his mischievous look and groaned as hard as Creepy.

Rachel gave her brother a blistering stare.

Eric threw up is hands in surrender. "Hey, I was only kidding! It was just an idea anyway ..."

We returned to deliberating more *serious* ways to wake him, but in the end we needn't have bothered. His eyes finally opened and this time they stayed open.

He blinked about thirty times as he tried to comprehend his predicament. "You hit me?" he said slowly, focusing on Eric. "Why did you hit me?"

We all exchanged glances. I mean, was that the stupidest question ever asked, or what?

"Because," Eric said, "you were going to kill them."

Mr. Creepy realized he was tied up. He wriggled for an instant and then gave up and laughed weakly. "I was not going to kill you. Why did you tie me up?"

"Why do you have a gun?" Rachel said.

He shook his head slowly and smiled. "Water. Please."

Rachel poured some water into his mouth and he gulped it down eagerly. He closed his eyes and sighed.

"So why do you have a gun?" I repeated.

"Protection," he whispered, his eyes still shut.

"From what?" Rachel asked.

When his eyes opened again, he seemed a lot more alert. "Do you know what the oldest profession in the world is?"

I shook my head, and wondered if maybe Eric

had whacked him too hard.

Eric rolled his eyes. "Cook?" he guessed.

Rachel and I snorted.

"What?" Eric sounded offended. "Someone had to cook the dinosaur meat back in the caveman days."

Our prisoner laughed too – a hearty laugh that relaxed me. His health was improving with each minute and I could now safely delete 'murder' from my mental rap sheet.

"No," he said. "Long before the first hunters, trappers, and cooks, grave robbers were at work."

None of us had a clue what he was talking about, so we didn't say anything.

"For ten thousand years it has been a common practice to bury the dead with objects they cherished while living. Weapons, jewelry, and other items of value were routinely buried with the bodies of the once living. And as long as this has been happening, looters have come to steal the artifacts. Do you understand?"

Rachel twisted her mouth as she thought this over. "So, you're a grave robber – a relic hunter?"

The man laughed and groaned at the same time. "No," he said. "But I go to locations where looters or other suspicious people might be present."

He looked at each of our faces for some sign of comprehension, but I don't think he saw any because he sighed and continued his explanation. "I have the gun to protect myself from those who wish to profit from the theft and sale of rare pieces of history – antiquities."

"But why are you *here*?" I asked. "Why are *you* in Sultana?"

He nodded. "My employers sent me for two reasons." He closed his eyes and paused for several seconds, like he was waiting for a wave of pain to pass. "I am here to investigate the authenticity of the object which was found near the river. And more importantly, I am here to protect any *genuine* archaeological discoveries from those who may wish to profit from them."

We considered what he had said while he closed his eyes and rested. Talking seemed to drain his energy. Everything he told us was certainly possible, but I wasn't feeling convinced, and from the looks on Eric and Rachel's faces, they weren't either.

"Hey," Eric said. He waited for his eyes to open before continuing. "Why would you fly here to investigate the plaque when experts from your country are already checking it out?"

He took a slow, deep breath and collected his thoughts before speaking. "Dr. Habib el-Medina is the foremost authority on ancient Egypt, but sometimes he gets too caught up with glorifying the achievements of his people and doesn't investigate the possibility of a hoax properly. In this case, he was overwhelmed by the idea that Egyptians may have discovered America, and he doesn't want to consider that the tablet – *your* tablet – could be a fake."

I ignored the fact that he knew we had made the plaque. "You said that you were also here to protect actual artifacts. Right?"

He nodded.

"Do you expect us to believe someone would come to Sultana to steal that tablet?"

He smiled like a guy who knew Spider-man's true identity. "You don't think your plaque is worth stealing?"

I shrugged and waited for him to continue.

"At this afternoon's press conference, there were two German news reporters. Did you see them?"

Our heads bobbed in unison.

"Well, they were *not* reporters. They are known throughout the world as thieves and dealers of antiquities. They are suspected of stealing rare pieces of history from Mexico, Brazil, Iran, and many other countries."

I stared at him in shock. The story was getting so bizarre I was starting to believe the guy.

Rachel moved the bottle toward Creepy's mouth. When he opened it, she poured more water inside. "Why didn't they try and steal it then?" she asked.

"Thank you," he said, licking water from his lips. "They did try. They wanted to turn off all the lights at the town meeting – in the hall. They were hoping that they could snatch the tablet and run while everyone was confused and in the dark."

I thought back to the press conference and how desperately the Germans had wanted access to the extension cords. Probably hoping Mr. Baker would simply point them to the electrical room – which he had.

"So why didn't they do it?" Rachel asked.

He grinned. "Because I was blocking the door, because I have a gun, and because they know me."

Eric looked incredulous. "They know you?"

"Of course they know me." He looked insulted. "I am Aubey Benchouchou." He said his name like he was a movie star.

Eric giggled. "Your name is Big Choo-Choo?"

Big Choo-Choo ignored Eric and said, "Please untie me – and we'll talk about your prize."

We all froze.

"What prize?" I said.

"Release me and I'll tell you. I promise I won't hurt you."

"What prize?" Rachel asked again.

If he could have, I bet he would've thrown his

hands in the air. "A heated but friendly debate has been ongoing since the discovery of your plaque last week. Half the members of my organization believed the tablet was authentic, while the other half was sure evidence would emerge proving it was a fake."

We huddled closer to each other, anxious and excited.

"The discovery has so consumed and amused the board, emergency meetings have been held every day since. If the object is real, it will, of course, cause all history books to be altered. On the other hand, if the plaque is part of a hoax, then those responsible would be awarded for their audacity. In the end, the board decided that if this finding passes all five of their tests, and is at any time thereafter declared a hoax, a cash prize of twenty-five thousand U.S. dollars will be awarded."

Eric was quick to gasp. "Whoa! Twenty-five thousand dollars. That's a lot of cash!"

Rachel was more cautious. "Did our tablet pass the tests?" She poured the last of the water into his mouth.

"Yes," he said after he had swallowed. "The discovery had to be reported on both BBC and CNN, and it was. The story had to appear in *The New York Times*, *The Los Angeles Times*, and *The London Times*, and it has. The finding had to be identified as authentic by at least two experts – it has. And the pranksters have to be found, and have to admit to it. You *do* admit to creating the tablet, correct?"

"Sure," Eric said.

"Yeah, we did it," I said.

"Wait a minute," Rachel cut in. "You said there were five tests."

"Ah, yes. For the final test you must provide proof that you are responsible for crafting the object. Will you please untie me now?"

"Proof?" Eric said, ignoring his request.

"Yes. Photographs or a video of you making the plaque would be ideal."

"What about the clay?" Rachel pointed to the trench. "This is where we got it."

"Perhaps, but anyone can come here and take clay. I need to check if that's okay – but you'll have to let me go first."

"How are you going to do that?" I asked.

"I have a cell phone in my jacket pocket. I'll call and find out if this will pass the fifth test. Now, *please* release me."

We untied one arm, and warned him that we would club him again if he tried anything. The three of us watched from a safe distance as he fumbled to find his phone with his free hand. Eric stood at the ready with a piece of lumber in case he had another weapon stashed on him. Big Choo-Choo looked at us with an amused expression. I guess three kids didn't really scare him.

He found the phone and pulled it free. The effort seemed to exhaust him and he took several deep breaths before he made the call. Finally, he dialed some place that must have had thirty numbers, and again, we had to wait for an answer. When at last he began talking, it was in Egyptian – I mean, Arabic. And we had no way of knowing what he was saying. For all we knew, he could have been calling for reinforcements.

The discussion sounded lively, but I couldn't tell if that was good or bad. After five minutes, he snapped the phone shut and rested it on his lap.

He shook his head. "I am sorry. The board's decision is final. They can't issue the award to you unless you can give definitive, physical evidence of your involvement. Now, please untie me."

CHAPTER 18

"You mean," I said, trying to understand the whole situation, "if we can prove to you that we made the plaque, those people you just called will give us twenty-five thousand dollars?"

"No," he said. "Now please let me go."

Eric looked like he wanted to club the guy again. "What do you mean, 'no'? You just said –"

He held up his free hand, interrupting Eric. "*I* will give you the money. Untie me now. *Please*." His face looked red with frustration or exposure to the sun, probably a little of both. He was starting to look like he wished he *had* shot us.

Rachel's eyes grew big. "*You're* going to give us the money?"

"Yes." He rubbed the back of his neck. "I was trying to tell you this but then *he* hit me." He pointed an accusing finger at Eric. "I have the check with me now."

I watched in horror as he tapped his jacket, just as he had an hour earlier above the trench. I thought he had been pointing to his gun, when he had actually been referring to our prize.

We had clobbered the guy for nothing! I was starting to feel a little bad for hitting him and for thinking he had been the bad guy all along.

Rachel furrowed her brow. "But you still can't give us the money without proof? Right?"

"Correct." Aubey gritted his teeth. "Will you let me go now?"

"What if we show you how we made the plaque?" Rachel asked. "We can show you the slate we used, the tools we used to carve the glyphs – everything."

"I'm sorry," he said. And he actually looked sorry, even though we were starting to annoy him. I was a little surprised, considering we had almost killed him.

"That's still too inconclusive," he explained. "Anyone could duplicate your tablet, and claim they were the original creators."

We were getting frustrated too. I mean, here was a guy ready to give us twenty-five grand, and all we had to do was prove we made the plaque – which we really did make.

Think, Cody. Think.

I stood up, rammed my hands in my pocket, and joined Eric in his pacing. Something cold and hard scraped my fingernails, and I pulled whatever it was out to examine it.

Holy smokes!

I had totally forgotten about the fragment we had broken off from the tablet – the fragment I was supposed to bury in the washout. This had to be proof! I felt like I was holding a winning lottery ticket.

I showed him the chunk and explained how we had broken it off the larger piece, intended to bury it, but then forgot about it. He took the chip and examined the symbols.

"As a final test," he said, "in order to prove to me that you did not find this at the river, tell me what is inscribed here."

It was our turn to laugh.

"Tuthmosis," I said proudly. And then to really show I knew my stuff, I added, "King of Upper and Lower Egypt during the Eighteenth Dynasty."

"Which was," Rachel added, grinning, "during the New Kingdom, around fifteen hundred B.C."

Aubey Benchouchou looked impressed. "I am convinced," he answered firmly, "And I assure you that you'll get the prize money. As soon as you let me go."

"Not so fast." Eric crossed his arms and tried his best to intimidate Aubey. "Let's see the check."

Aubey glowered at Eric. I thought I even heard a growl escape his throat. Finally, his shoulders slumped and he gave in. "Reach into my jacket pocket. There you'll find an envelope, and in it is a certified check for the amount of twenty-five thousand dollars."

None of us moved. Not even Eric.

"Fine," he said. "I'll take out the check. But please do not hit me." He dramatically inserted his hand into his jacket and pulled out the envelope.

Rachel snatched it from him and quickly pulled out a piece of paper the size of a dollar bill. "It looks real," she said, showing it to us. "But I've never seen a real ..."

"– How come no names are on it?" Eric said, examining the paper.

"Because," Aubey said, speaking through clenched teeth, "you tried to kill me before I could issue the check in your names."

We considered this for a moment.

"Maybe you better call your bosses one more time," I said, not wanting any complications. "Just to make sure it's okay with them."

He shook his head emphatically, but reached for his phone anyway. I should probably have felt guilty, but this was twenty-five thousand dollars we were talking about!

We waited impatiently for him to get the green light to give us the check. I was relieved at first because his conversation seemed to be civil and polite. But then after five minutes of debating, he became agitated and even started whining.

My hands were damp with sweat. What if they

said "no" and wouldn't give us the prize money? What if he was telling his bosses we tied him up and tried to kill him? The money would solve all our problems. If we got the money, Eric and Rachel would definitely not need to move.

I had a strange feeling in my gut. On the one hand I felt guilty that our hoax caused so much trouble – and maybe even a concussion. But on the other hand our plan worked because my best friend wouldn't have to move away now.

I always wanted the scheme to succeed, but I never imagined we would actually be rewarded for being the perpetrators of a hoax. And with twenty-five thousand dollars too! I tried dividing the money equally and came up with something like eight thousand dollars each. But he said the money was in U.S. dollars, so that meant that –

"– The board has imposed two additional conditions and then you can get your prize," Aubey said. He collapsed his phone in half and threw it on the ground next to him.

"What conditions?" Rachel was suspicious again.

"You must make a public apology for attempting to mislead the scientists and your community."

I quickly weighed the consequences of being grounded and having to make an embarrassing public apology against the fact my *two* best friends

– because Rachel was like a friend now too – would no longer have to move. It was a no-brainer. "I agree," I said.

Eric squinted at me and Rachel. Then he shrugged his shoulders and said, "Sure, whatever."

"And?" Rachel asked. "What's the second condition?"

Aubey Benchouchou wriggled uncomfortably, and for the first time that afternoon, he looked like he'd rather we had killed him. "You have to come with me to Cairo as guests, so that you may properly appreciate the achievements of the early Egyptians." I watched as either a tear or a bead of sweat rolled down his cheek. "Now, for the love of Allah, please untie me."

CHAPTER 19

We did untie him.

And that same evening we met our first condition and apologized.

I was surprised we didn't get into that much trouble. Mom and Dad grounded me, but I like to think that was only because they had to – so they'd look like responsible parents. They seemed to enjoy the attention as much as everyone else in Sultana. Dad even whispered to me that he sold more gas in those two days than he had in two months!

The TV crews stayed long enough to make a story out of the hoax and then trickled away. Professor Bell's team from the university said they would have discovered the hoax anyway after conducting further tests. *Sure, sure*! And Dr. Habib el-Medina was too embarrassed to even show up to the second press conference. He slipped out of Sultana without a word.

Eric and Rachel's share of the huge prize made Mrs. Summers forgive the prank after an initial uproar. Business at the Rivercrest Motel & Restaurant continued to improve even after we confessed, and she didn't get fired. She never spoke of moving again. The owner even joked about having a gigantic reproduction of our tablet made as a town monument to keep the people coming.

Now *that* would be cool!

The community service the R.C.M.P. imposed on us for causing public mischief wasn't *too* bad. They said we each had to do fifty hours of public service in Sultana. But the only thing that ever needed doing was picking up garbage around town and mowing the grass in the small graveyard behind the Rivercrest. And because of all the new business there, the owner felt sorry for us and *paid* us – secretly, of course – to do the work. So, you see, we kind of got summer jobs out of the hoax too.

Reporters visited Sultana throughout the summer, just to see the place – and the kids – that had caused all the fuss. In fact, I think they enjoyed writing about how we fooled everyone as much as they enjoyed the original discovery. Our story was printed in eight newspapers along with photographs of us holding our tablet, which the university returned to us. It was almost like they didn't want it anywhere near them – like it was cursed.

Finally, after all the grounding, the community service, and the reporters, we made it to an airport in Egypt. And when we landed in Cairo, Rachel surprised me with an overenthusiastic hug.

Looking back now, she probably shouldn't have done that. Because Aubey – our chaperone for the trip – got distracted when Eric shouted, "Oh, gross!", and then those German thieves from the community hall jumped us while Aubey wasn't looking, and ...

But I'll tell you about that next time.

ABOUT THE AUTHOR:

Andreas Oertel was born in Germany and has spent most of his life in Manitoba, Canada. Fascinated by archaeology, ancient civilizations, and discovery, he can often be found exploring the local beaches with his trusty metal detector. Andreas lives in Lac du Bonnet in Eastern Manitoba. He is also the author of the young adult novel *Deep Trouble* (Write Words Inc., 2008).